T0208041

IMMINENT DEMISE

IMMINENT DEMISE

A NOVEL

JIM STRATTON

IMMINENT DEMISE
A NOVEL

iUniverse books may be ordered through booksellers or by contacting:

iUniverse
1663 Liberty Drive
Bloomington, IN 47403
www.iuniverse.com
1-800-Authors (1-800-288-4677)

ISBN: 978-1-5320-6180-6 (sc)
ISBN: 978-1-5320-6179-0 (e)

Library of Congress Control Number: 2018914061

Print information available on the last page.

iUniverse rev. date: 11/27/2018

Contents

This work is dedicated to my wife Rebecca, who has an insatiable appetite for reading novels. I promised her that I would write one for her, and since she has read so many, I anxiously await her critique of my work compared to those she has read.

I would also like to thank my daughter, Dr. Jennifer Do and Rebecca for many hours of proof reading.

Happiness is an elusive state of existence. Some believe it is found within a context of having material wealth, everything they ever dreamed of, and enough money to stave off any worry about attaining what they want.

Others think that it is hidden under some formula that can be uncovered only by psychiatric probing of the inner self and what was passed down through genetic makeup from prior generations.

Many people feel that their faith provides all their needs. Others believe true happiness will not be achieved in this life, that this life is but a training ground for the afterlife.

It is obvious to me that true happiness has nothing to do with material possessions. It is not found in satisfying some inner questioning or even in fulfilling some lifetime goal.

Could it be that the simple parts of life, the uncomplicated things, and those things that spring up as pleasant memories and comforting dreams outline the happiness we all seem to be in search of for most of our lives?

Could it be that our service to others, our love for our families and fellow human beings, and the chores in our day-to-day lives that are kin to commitment and are lasting are the real keys to finding a satisfaction that can make all the difficulties and challenges of this existence easier to bear?

Could it be that happiness can be found in simply serving others and recognizing that special feeling that comes from doing so?

I submit to you that if we all see that the simple, quiet aspects of life provide the most substance, then we can concentrate on bringing about the change in our society that will make happiness more attainable for all people.

Our certain and imminent demise is not always at the end of a long, full life, but the time we do have can be meaningful and worthwhile.

Some of the characters in my story found the path that leads to love, the cornerstone of happiness. Others met their end still searching for some tangible reason to live at all.

This work is not intended to be filled with the acts of super heroes. It is about everyday people who despite extraordinary circumstances, manage to live lives worth living in a world inundated by the overstated and overrated hype of modern media.

Chapter 1

Layout of the Land

Certainly, there was more to Elliot Timberlake than most people in his home town saw. He was, after all, a handsome young man of twenty-six, fresh out of college and law school, and by all the standards of his day, an eligible bachelor. He stood six feet one and had the build of an athlete, although he had never been involved in organized sports. His hazel eyes, wavy dark brown hair, and sun-darkened complexion seemed to attract all sorts of inquisitions from the local bevy of beautiful and likewise available women.

It was obvious that he could be the great and shining star you see in the movies or anything he wanted to be in this life. He had that kind of stature about him, but he was humble and that came across to everyone he met.

Despite his good looks and appeal to the opposite sex, Elliot had a shyness that kept him from being bold and direct in his dating life. That actually may have added to his allure. It gave him a humility and kindness that was lacking in society.

Elliot had majored in criminal law, but now, two years out of school, he was still working odd jobs in Eldsboro, Ohio. He had been born there, but he had moved away at the age of fourteen, when his father died in a car crash, and his mother moved back to her hometown of Williston, Missouri.

It was only after law school that Elliot came back to his hometown, which had grown to a population of about twenty-five thousand by the time he returned. He had planned to get settled in his home town and take the bar exam, but life kept getting in the way. For now, he was perfectly content to make enough money to maintain his small home place. There was still plenty of time for attaining whatever measure of wealth he decided would make him happy.

Elliot kept to himself after work each day. He busied himself by working a small farm about a mile south of town. Now, that may seem a little odd for a young man with a degree in criminal law, but he had another vision for his life that did not necessarily align with that education. In fact, Elliot went down the road to his study of law to please his mom. She had hounded him about making money to ensure his place in the grand scheme of things. He never really wanted to be part of the rat race. He wanted one day to own a large self-sustaining farm that would provide him with everything from vegetables and fruit to milk and beef from herds of cattle.

He often reasoned that he would probably be forced to complete his bar exam and practice law, if he was to realize his dreams of a much larger farm, but for now, the status quo was plenty.

It was spring, and this part of Ohio was green and lush. It was warm, and plenty of rain had jump-started Elliot's crop of vegetables. His one-acre garden drew compliments from the entire neighborhood. It would be a pleasant chore in a month or two to be able to harvest some of the fruits of his labor.

The garden still needed attention. There were weeds to eliminate, bugs to exterminate, and larger animals like rabbits, squirrels, and even deer to discourage from eating the plants before they produced. The entire garden had a lace-like chicken wire fence that was about six feet high but was neatly kept like all of Elliot's property. Taking care of things was something Elliot got an old-time pleasure out of doing each day.

And that is exactly what Elliot was doing late one afternoon after working at the nearby sawmill all day. He was attired in his overalls, no shirt, and a pair of old sneakers that looked as though they had been through a couple of world wars.

Some little noise caught his attention. He could not tell at first where the noise came from. Perhaps it was one of the many white-tailed deer that frequently ambled by to sample some of the fresh acorns in the woods just beyond the back fence. He slowly lifted his head and leaned on his rake to behold a strikingly beautiful young lady approaching the garden from the woods at the far end of the property.

"Hello!" she called. "I am Lily … Lily Owens. I was hiking and saw this exquisite garden and just had to see it closer. I hope you don't mind."

"No, no, no, not at all," Elliot replied. "Come on over. There is a gate just to your left at the corner."

He thought about how he was dressed and got a little squeamish, as he realized that he was in the presence of a truly gorgeous young woman with a face like an angel and a walk like a spirit gliding across the ground.

"I apologize for my appearance, but I didn't really expect company." He scrambled to dust off his overalls.

"Don't you worry at all about that. I don't mind a bit." Lily looked around and saw all the neatly arranged and perfectly tended plants. She smiled and said, "It is a great garden. Maybe I could come by at a better time, when you are more prepared for company."

"Well, yes, yes. Why don't you do that? When can you come? I mean, just give me a call sometime, and we can set up a time," stammered Elliot.

"Okay, I will do that. What's your number?" she asked.

Elliot told her his cell phone number, she put it into her phone, and Elliot took her number down in his. Lily turned slowly away and disappeared into the woods at about the same place she'd come out a few minutes before, and Elliot raked his way to the end of the row, put his chin on the rake, and stared for several minutes into the woods just wondering. Yes, just wondering. She was really, really pretty. He recalled her long, flowing black hair that fell in long curves over her shoulders and half covered her hauntingly blue eyes which were perfectly set off with eye lashes that curved smoothly, accentuating the luster of her hair. He thought of her lips as she spoke. Her words seemed to be visible as they came toward him.

His mind raced and became confused. Lily became all he could think about until he went on to other chores around the farm. He would work for a few minutes and then stop and think about Lily for a few minutes. When he finally finished his chores, he went inside his neat-as-a-pin cottage.

He could not bring himself to even interview for what would probably be available jobs with law firms in town, so Elliot had taken several odd jobs since he had been back in Eldsboro. Most of them were seasonal and lasted for a few months, and then he was forced to go on to another. Although he found plenty of work this way, he knew he would never save enough money to buy that land he hoped for by continuing on this path. He decided that, for now at least, he would keep his law degree as a back-up instead of his main objective.

He made friends quite easily, but he was not particularly outgoing, and word of mouth kept him aware of the jobs that were available. So, it came to pass that he landed a steady job working at the saw mill. He didn't particularly like it, but it kept a roof over his head and food on the table.

In the days that followed, Elliot's work at the saw mill became more and more unbearable. His duties there were mostly manual labor, as one would expect such as unloading the many logging trucks that came through the gates with alarming regularity. He sometimes filled in at the debarking operation, but his daydreams often caused an inattentiveness that made both jobs dangerous not only for him but for those working with and around him.

One afternoon, right after lunch break, Elliot's thoughts took his mind completely off of his fork truck driving, and he almost ran over the shift supervisor.

He brought the equipment to a stop immediately, hopped off the truck and ran over to Mr. Felton. "I'm so sorry, Mr. Felton. Are you Okay?"

"Dang you, Elliot!" roared Dan Felton. "Where is your head these days? I want to see you right after work in my office and don't be late!"

"Yes, Mr. Felton. I'm awfully sorry. I promise it won't happen again. I will be there at three o'clock."

"Well, see that it doesn't, and see that you are!" Mr. Felton snapped.

Elliot had been at his position for more than a year and had been a good worker, except for these occasional lapses of concentration.

The rest of his shift was uneventful, and the time came to meet Mr. Felton at his office. Elliot feared that his mistakes might make this the end of the line for him.

I need this job, he thought. *But it is just a stepping-stone. I am not going to let that louse Felton take it away from me. I will just bite my tongue and not get angry and caught up in whatever he says.*

He climbed the two flights of steps and proceeded across the catwalk that led to the office.

Mr. Felton's secretary, Eleanor Malone recognized Elliot and said, "Go right in. He's expecting you."

With some trepidation, Elliot opened the door.

Mr. Felton told him to come in and sit down, although he was facing the opposite direction in his high-back leather chair. Elliot could only see the back of his head and his right hand on the arm of the chair. The smoke from his cigar rose into the air from his opposite hand.

Elliot eased into the straight-back chair in front of the desk and waited for Mr. Felton to continue.

Suddenly, the big chair rotated one hundred and eighty degrees, so that the two were face-to -face.

"I just have one question for you Timberlake. Do you need this job at all?" Mr. Felton inquired.

Elliot nodded.

"Well, it surely doesn't look like it to me." he continued. "Well, I'm not going to fire you for almost running me over out there, but I do declare that if you don't get your mind on your work, the next time I call you in … you will be outta here. Okay then, get back to work!"

Elliot went back to his job site to finish up a few things that he neglected to do, because of the meeting with Mr. Felton.

I guess the old fuss box is right, in a way, Elliot thought. *If I am going to stay with this job for whatever time I need to, I should concentrate better and give it my best. I don't like Felton, but he does have a point, I suppose.*

He punched out and walked through the gate and into the parking lot, where his truck was parked. He got in, put the key in the ignition, but he did not start the engine. Instead, he just sat there pondering what had happened during the day and where his life was leading him.

There was certainly no real future for him in the lumber company. He did not particularly like the atmosphere of the place, and he absolutely disliked his association with Mr. Felton. He silently wished he could get out of there soon and began to consider going ahead with law school and the bar exam.

He sat there in the truck for almost a half hour, before he finally came out of his trance-like state and cranked the engine of his old truck and started home. A little smile came to his face, as he once thought about Lily and when he might be able to see her again.

Chapter 2

The Next Encounter

After the incident at the saw mill, Elliot settled into a routine of hard work, safe and stable habits, and, most of all, a better attitude about his job.

He was a model employee for the company after that incident and was rewarded with a promotion that gave him not only a better salary but more pride in what he was doing. *Now that I am moving up, maybe I can move even higher into management and own that farm someday.*

He began to mix more socially with the Eldsboro townspeople. When it came time for the company fall party, Elliot actually decided to go. He put on his only sports coat, a tie, and his best blue jeans and showed up to see some of his new friends.

He didn't expect to see her, but Elliot still remembered exactly how Lily looked from their meeting in his garden. He hoped he might see her again and get better acquainted, but there were really no expectations on his part, especially at the company get-together. It had been several weeks since they had seen each other, but he had begun to compare every girl he met or passed on the street to his vision of Lily.

Elliot had pretty much resigned himself to letting Lily make the first move if a relationship with her was in the cards. He was quite shy when it came to relationships with women. He had pulled up her phone number several times, but he could not make the call. From the first time he saw her, he had wondered whether she might just be the one to make his life complete, but it seemed like something magical would have to happen to get them together.

Elliot said hello to several of the guys from work and was even cordial to Ms. Malone and Mr. Felton. He walked over to the table filled with drinks and hors d'oeuvres and filled his plate with a sampling of all the fixings. He sensed someone to his left and looked up to see none other than Lily intently choosing her food without a glance upward.

She looked like a princess to Elliot in her pink chiffon gown. Her hair was pinned back tightly into a shiny ball that luminesced in the colored lights of the dining hall. Her high-heeled shoes matched her skin tone so closely that it appeared as though she was shoeless, standing on her tiptoes. A pearl necklace adorned her modestly cut neckline, and matching earrings hung down to almost touch her shoulders.

Elliot was so struck with her beauty that he could barely utter, "Lily, is that you?"

Lily turned to face him, and her surprise and delight to see him was evident. Elliot saw that delight as a sparkle in her eyes he had not seen before. "It is Elliot, isn't it? Elliot Timberlake … right?"

"Yes." replied Elliot. "Are you with the sawmill?"

"Not exactly." she replied. "I came with Mr. Felton. I'm kind of his date, I guess you could say."

"Oh." Elliot said with an obvious disappointment in his voice.

That leaves me out for sure. Felton is a much better catch than me, but gosh, there is such a wide gap in their ages.

"Well, I guess I had better be going. I have a long day in front of me tomorrow."

"But, you just got here, didn't you?" prompted Lily. "I saw you come in just a few minutes ago."

Elliot did not pick up on the situation right away, but Lily had obviously been acting surprised to see him at the table just before.

She saw him come in and purposely/accidentally bumped into him there.

"Yes, that's right, but I just dropped in to say hi to some of the guys I work with." Elliot said. "I had better go now. I have to work tomorrow, and there are lots of things to do in my garden. I have to get ready to harvest some of the vegetables soon."

Lily shook her head in acknowledgement of Elliot's comment. "And don't forget that you said it would be okay if I came over to see that garden a little closer one day, too."

"Yes, I remember." replied Elliot. "I will call you soon, and we will set up a time. I have your number. Take care."

They exchanged glances and separated to go in opposite directions.

Mr. Felton approached from the dance floor, where he had been sampling the sashaying styles of three or four of the attractive ladies who were more than happy to spend time with the company Casanova. Mr. Felton did not look the part, but he had a way of making promises that made his womanizing ways and overbearing demeanor not so apparent.

He walked on up to Lily, threw his heavy arm around her waist, and pulled her close to his side. Felton was a large man and forceful in all aspects of his life.

Lily was becoming more and more annoyed at his physical nature. She thought, *He had better ease up, or I am going to push back.*

"What were you and young Timberlake talking about?" Felton asked.

Lily, a little taken back at what seemed to be an impertinent question said, "Just saying hello, I guess."

"Well, you don't need to be talking at all to him, okay?" Mr. Felton snapped.

His first name was Daniel, but Lily who had just met him a few weeks before, called him Dan at his request.

"Look, Dan. I told you he was just being polite." Lily said with elevated volume and a snarl on her face. "And besides, I'll talk to anyone I like. You're not my boss. I don't work for you, and we're not married, either."

"You're out with me, aren't you?" queried Mr. Felton.

"Yes, Dan." replied Lily "But it will be the last time, if you give me an ultimatum like that again."

"Mighty uppity all of a sudden aren't you, Ms. Owens?" Mr. Felton added. "It might be a good idea for you to remember that I know something about your precious little brother that could get him into a lot of hot water, if the right people found out about it."

All Lily could think about from that point on was that Mr. Felton had told her that Johnny had started the fire down at the high school.

Lily's shoulders slumped a bit and she dropped her head as Mr. Felton led her back to the dance floor. Lily felt like a wet noodle as they attempted to waltz through the maze of couples. It became more and more uncomfortable for her. She attempted to distance herself from his constantly pulling her close to him.

Finally, he said, "Okay, why don't I just take you home. You're no good to me this way, anyhow."

He grabbed her wrist and all but pulled her off the dance floor and out of the building. They got into his black Lincoln sedan and sped away in a cloud of Ohio dust.

Lily lived south of town, about three miles out, and the drive home took them right past Elliot's farm. She noticed that the lights were still on at the farm house, which was no surprise, since it was only about nine o'clock on a Saturday night.

Mr. Felton pulled in front of Lily's parents' house and tried to kiss her and failed, as she hastily exited the car.

"Well, alright then," he blurted. "But you remember what I said earlier about your brother. I will call you tomorrow."

Don't bother! Lily thought as she sneered back at him almost tripping over the doorstep. She said, "I think I will just let you think about things for a while. When you cool off, you may call me in a week or two. I might talk to you then, and I might just not."

Mr. Felton drove away erratically.

But, she didn't go in right away. She lingered on the stoop. She saw him out of the corner of her eye but paid little attention. She just leaned against the overhang column and gazed longingly at the half moon that was peeking in and out of the clouds.

She started humming "Are You Lonesome Tonight?" and wondered what Elliot might be doing at home. *Is he making a sandwich? He certainly did not eat very much at the party.* She remembered that she had his phone number in her phone.

Should I … or shouldn't I? she thought.

"I should!" she shouted out aloud suddenly to herself.

She bolted through the front door, right past her mom and dad who were sitting on the couch watching television. Up the stairs she went hitting only every other step.

Her dad William and mom Nancy yelled out almost simultaneously, "Lily, what's wrong?"

They heard her mumble "Nothing," as she disappeared at the top of the stairs. Into the room she went, slamming the door behind her. *I will talk to my parents about it later.*

She retrieved her cell phone out of her purse faster than Matt Dillon drawing his six- shooter from his holster on *Gunsmoke*. She found Elliot's number and was about to press the button to call him, when thoughts of that awful man and his threats ran through her mind. She hesitated again. She wondered *what could Felton could do to me and Johnny? After all, it was Johnny's word against Mr. Felton's. Johnny is the star of the Eldsboro football team. No one would believe that he had started that fire at the school's machine shop. Besides, Mr. Felton only had second hand information from someone who said they saw him do it.*

The day after the fire, Johnny had confessed to Lily that he knew who had started the fire. It was Felton's own nephew, Ricky Pendleton. Johnny and Ricky were best friends, and the code of ethics among friends is that you don't rat on each other.

Ricky had received a bad grade from the Machine Shop instructor, because he was habitually late, and he purposely dropped a match into the oily rags bin. He didn't think it would be any more than that, but it got out of hand, and the entire shop burned to the ground.

Ricky panicked when Mr. Felton confronted him about the fire and shifted the blame to Johnny. Mr. Felton carried a lot of weight around the community, and everyone with any knowledge of what had happened kept quiet.

As Lily pondered the possibilities and consequences, she decided against calling Elliot. She put on her pajamas, crawled into bed, and endured a restless night.

The next morning, Lily heard her cell phone ringing as she was getting into the shower. It was only eight o'clock, and she really didn't feel like answering it, but she did.

It was Mr. Felton.

"Hey Lily ... it's Dan. What about driving out to the lake with me? The boat is fueled up and ready to go."

"I don't think so," returned Lily. "You treated me pretty bad last night. I think I will go to church this morning."

"Church? Aw, come on, Lil. I am sorry about last night. I'll pick you up in an hour, and we'll have a blast!"

"I said no. I am going to church like I told you." Lily said. "Mom and Dad are going, and I sort of promised them last week that I would go with them."

Lily knew that Mr. Felton finally got the message when he said a grumpy good-bye.

Lily finished her shower and had breakfast with her parents, who questioned her briefly about the night before. Lily offered little explanation, and they dropped the subject.

The ride to church was quiet except for Ms. Owens usual rhetoric about how the Ladies' Auxiliary couldn't decide on the color scheme for the upcoming bazaar.

Finally, Mr. Owens interrupted, "Lily, what's with you and Mr. Felton? I know we have covered this ground before, but I just don't get what you see in that old buzzard. He is too old for you!"

Lily, knowing that she should tell him about the situation, said, "Dad, I can't explain it now, but one day soon, I will fill you in on all the details. Dan is being a real pest, but I will figure out a way to deal with him. Just be patient and trust me, okay?"

"Sure, Lily. Just be careful. I don't trust him as far as I could throw a Volkswagen Beetle," Mr. Owens replied.

Lily was not a devout Christian like her parents, but she did believe in treating her fellow human beings with dignity and kindness. Her parents had set a great example for her growing up, and now she was a very mature twenty-three-year-old and was well thought of in her community. She had a great job at the veterinary clinic and was happy with her work there. The association with the much older Mr. Felton might have been the downfall of someone with less integrity.

Mr. and Mrs. Owens followed Lily into the sanctuary and sat next to her on the front row pew. Reverend Malakai Johnson strolled over to the pulpit from his velvet-covered chair near the choir loft, cleared his throat, and opened his tattered Bible to the bookmark he had placed there during his last study session.

He stared at the text for several seconds and then looked up slowly and scanned the congregation from right to left and then the opposite way. He put his hands in front of him equal-distant on each side of the book and began his sermon.

"Today!" he shouted loud enough to wake the dead in in the cemetery. "Today, you will make many decisions that will change your life, and some will affect those around you, maybe forever!"

"We make thousands of decisions each day. Will I have that fourth double-dipped chocolate-covered peanut? Do I need to blink right now? I have an itchy nose. Should I scratch it now? What street do I take on the way home today? Most are simple decisions that take no real time from your gray matter, but some will be rehashed in your mind for days, months, or even years. Some decisions are black and white which our conscience helps us differentiate."

"One of those decisions will be to either tell the truth or submit to the ruler of the darkness, old Satan himself … and lie." He continued. "Lies come in many forms. They can be the out-and-out kind or little white lies, and yes even lies of omission … hiding the truth. All of these are still lying, and they go against the very fabric of what Christianity is."

Lily had paid little attention to the few sermons she had heard over the past months, but these words broke through her clouded thinking. She thought about Elliot and Mr. Felton, and suddenly, she was quite interested in the words of the preacher.

Reverend Johnson continued, "Our modern world commonly glosses over the evil of lies. We even make games about it. We watch television shows that actually reward people who lie the most convincingly. There are reality shows that glorify schemers and those who prey on the unsuspecting and less worldly."

"We are systematically being brainwashed into thinking that being honest, clean, and virtuous is boring and not at all socially acceptable-that deception that helps us gain what we want in this world is not sin at all but just means to an end."

Lily listened with a renewed awareness and waited for the next words from the persuasive speaker.

"The Bible tells us that the meek shall inherit the earth. It also tells us that we are to stand up for the Lord in our daily lives and to live by his commands. I tell you that we cannot and must not let the lies and deception of the serpent who deceived Adam and Eve in the Garden of Eden rule our lives. We must expose the real evil that causes life to be separate from God's Word."

Lily squirmed on the pew. Her dad noticed and looked over and gave her a perplexing snarl. Lily smiled back at him sheepishly and looked towards the pulpit. She had been taught to be reverent and attentive in church, and she got the point of his look.

What a fool I have been, she thought.

She focused on the last few words of the sermon with a stern resolve to make a stand against Mr. Felton.

Chapter 3

Trouble at the Mill

The next few weeks saw things get back to normal at the sawmill. Elliot continued to grow as a loyal employee and his skills in his new position. His promotion put him in charge of a small crew of two men and one woman who kept up with the inventory of all the mill's hardwood and softwood logs before and after debarking and being cut into planks and boards for shipping. It wasn't a particularly difficult task, but the sheer volume of materials made it time consuming and took up most of the crew's work week. The mill had undergone some automation, but this part of the operation was still mostly manual. All four filled in with other chores when not engaged in their primary responsibilities.

The job did something else for Elliot that was important to him. It kept him away from his old nemesis, Mr. Felton. He had much less direct contact with him, and that was just fine with Elliot. He just could not let go of the thought of that old codger being with Lily. He still could not figure out what hold he had over Lily or what she saw in him. Nonetheless, Elliot steered clear of them both out of respect for Lily.

One day, however, Mr. Felton walked up to Elliot and his crew in the mill yard. He seemed agitated, as he singled out Elliot.

"Timberlake, I need to talk to you now!" He barked. "I saw the numbers on finished lumber last week, and I don't like what I saw."

"Not sure I know what you mean by that," replied Elliot.

"I'll tell you what I mean," said Mr. Felton. "My bonus was thirty percent less last week than normal ... thirty percent!" He continued. "I know how many trucks come through that gate and how much wood is on each one of them. I've been at this mill for twenty-five years, and no young, wet-behind-the-ears college kid is going to take my money away from me."

"Mr. Felton, first of all I didn't even know that you got a bonus based on the volume coming into the plant," rebutted Elliot. "All I do is keep a record of what we debark and cut into usable product."

"I'm telling you that your numbers are wrong." Mr. Felton said. "You know what I think? I think you doctored those figures because you and I don't get along-and maybe, just maybe because you're jealous of me and Lily!"

"Jealous of you and Lily? I hardly even know her," Elliot said in a slightly elevated tone of voice. "You and Lily are of no concern to me."

"Well, I'm telling you that I won't stand for you messing with my paycheck. You had better start double checking the inventories. If my bonus keeps going down, you will be going down, too along with your three companions over there!" Mr. Felton yelled.

Elliot's crew overheard part of the conversation and exchanged glances with each other, and their faces showed some alarm at what Mr. Felton might do to them, if his accusations were true. After all, he had a lot of influence with the company and in the community as well.

Mr. Felton stormed away waving his fist in the air.

Elliot walked over to his crew and consoled them by telling them that he would take care of everything. He told them not to worry.

He decided that he would go to his supervisor the next week and ask to see the log books, so he could compare his numbers with the time before he became inventory chief to see whether there had been a big change in production versus raw materials.

That night, Elliot worked in his garden for a short while and went inside for a snack. He came back out to check the water and oil in his old pick-up truck. It wasn't much of a vehicle, but it got him from point A to point B reliably. He began to think seriously about buying a new truck, if the job at the mill kept going well.

Then, the sound of a rooster crowing came from his pocket. It was his cell phone signaling him to respond.

"Hello, Elliot. This is Lily. I hope I am not calling at a bad time."

"Not at all!" replied Elliot. "I was just doing a little preventive maintenance on my truck. What can I do for you?"

"Well, I thought maybe I might come over and get a closer look at that garden of yours. I mean, if it's not too much trouble. It looks even better than it did in the spring,"

"But, what about Mr. Felton?" asked Elliot. "Do you think he will be upset if you come over to my place?"

"I'm not worried about him. Besides, I just wanted to see that garden. I might want to buy a few of those tomatoes you are so famous for growing," said Lily. "And, to be quite honest, I need to talk to you about something."

"Okay then, if you say it is not a problem. When can you come over?" asked Elliot.

Lily replied, "How about tomorrow afternoon about four o'clock?"

"That would be great!" said Elliot trying to hide his excitement. "See you at four tomorrow…Bye."

Elliot hung up after saying good-bye and thought *I'd better straighten up the place, before Lily comes over tomorrow. She said she wanted to see the garden, but that was always as neat as a could be … not so much inside the house.* So, he concentrated on cleaning, putting away things, and just in case she might want some coffee, he readied the pot, so that all he would have to do is hit the start button to get it going. And, to be completely prepared, he placed a bottle of white wine in some ice inside the refrigerator.

I wonder what she needs to talk to me about?

He reasoned *it probably has something to do with Mr. Felton, but it might be something so simple as supplying her family's vegetable needs. No matter … I will find out tomorrow.*

The next morning at the mill, Elliot found it hard to concentrate on his work (as he did before) because of his date with Lily coming up later.

But, things were getting done until midway of the afternoon, when who should approach Elliot with his frock in a wad but old briny breath himself, Mr. Felton.

"Okay, Timberlake, it's time we had something out right here and now!" growled Felton. "What have you been telling Lily? Have you been seeing her behind my back?"

Elliot replied, "Mr. Felton, first of all if I did see her, it wouldn't be any of your business ... this is a free country, and I don't see a tag on her forehead saying *Felton's property*."

"Do you know that I can have you fired, you little idiot?" Lashed back Felton.

"Well, why don't you just try that, you **big** idiot!" Elliot said loudly. He was obviously getting more and more agitated each second by the inquisition. He had been trying his best to avoid conflict with Felton, but his interest in Lily was growing. He felt himself becoming bolder about standing up to the bully, even if Felton could hurt his standing at the mill. "I haven't done anything wrong, so back off, mister." he insisted.

"I've just about finished my investigation into your handling of the inventory records!" Mr. Felton shouted. "And by tomorrow, I'll have enough on you to hang you out to dry."

He walked away muttering to himself and slapping his hands together.

It was almost three o'clock, so Elliot finished up his work, signed his name in the log book, and left the plant with a renewed snap in his step, when he remembered that Lily would be coming by soon.

If Mr. Felton found out about Lily coming to his house, there would certainly be more trouble, but it would be worth it to spend time with Lily. He got home, took a quick shower, and put on his best slacks, his favorite navy-blue pull-over, brushed his teeth, gargled twice, and put on some comfortable but nice-looking loafers. He fluffed up the pillows on the sofa and hid a pair of socks he spotted at the last minute under the easy chair cushion just as he heard a car pull up in the driveway.

It was Lily. Elliot peeped through the drapes and watched her legs slide sideways out of her sporty, pale yellow Mustang. He stepped back and eased over to the front door, so that she would not have to wait long to come inside. In fact, he opened the door before she rang the doorbell.

His mind raced as Lily stepped up onto the doorstep. She was even more attractive than he remembered. Her peach-colored skirt was accented by a pale green blouse that ruffled around her neck. Her off-white high heel shoes were shiny. She put out her right hand to greet Elliot.

"Hello there," she said boldly. "How are you?"

"Oh, just fine Lily. Won't you come in?"

Without hesitation, she squeezed in past Elliot and the door jam, and he closed the door behind her. He ushered her into the den area and offered her a seat on the couch.

"I can't stay but a little while." Lily said as she sat down. "Let me get right to the point if I may. Elliot, I have a problem that I think only you can help me with this. It is about Mr. Felton."

"Me? Are you sure you need my help? After all, I hardly know you, and Mr. Felton and I are not exactly bosom buddies."

"Well, actually you touched on both reasons I wanted to see you today." replied Lily.

Lily's countenance showed worry. She tilted her head forward. The inside of her eyebrows angled towards her nose, and she squeezed her lips together. As Elliot listened intently, Lily began to tell him that there was something more sinister about her relationship with Dan Felton. They looked at each other and they both hesitated before continuing.

"It's like this Elliot. I have wanted to see you, er … go out with you, well since the first time we met. Remember, in your garden?'

"Of course, I remember, Lily, I just assumed after I saw you and Felton at the party that you were with him."

Lily explained that there was a lot more to the story than what Elliot knew. She told him about the extortion Felton was using against her because of her brother, Johnny's situation … that he kept threatening to turn Johnny in for starting the fire at the high school shop, if she did not keep seeing him.

"I just don't know what to do." She placed her hand on the back of Elliot's which was resting close to her on the couch.

"Why don't you just go to the police?" Elliot asked.

"I want to but do you know who the assistant police chief in Eldsboro is? It is Dan Felton's favorite cousin, George Conrad. Who do you think they would believe him or me? I can't take that chance."

"What about your mom and dad. Won't they help?" questioned Elliot. "And besides, did your brother start the fire, or didn't he?"

"He says he didn't, and I believe him."

By now, Lily's hand was gripped around Elliot's wrist so tightly that he reached over with his opposite hand and laid it on top of her hand, lifted it up, and held it between his.

He looked up into her dreamy eyes and asked how he could help. It would turn out to be a defining moment in his young life and Lily's.

"Well, first of all, I told Dan to stay away from me, but he keeps calling and threatening me about Johnny. I have decided to stand up to him, but without the help of the police, I feel like I am fighting a losing battle. He is a powerful man around here."

Lily explained that she thought that Elliot could help her get some evidence about Ricky's involvement in the fire. She felt that would be the only way to break the hold that Felton had on her for good. Then, she said, "I think Johnny could tell us what he knows and what he saw that night, to give us a starting point. Just one little thing might do it."

"Okay." Elliot said. "You talk to Johnny and let him know that I am helping you, so he won't get mad at me for interfering. Then, all three of us will get together to talk about it and come up with a plan."

Lily let out a sigh of relief. "I feel better about things now." It had been hard keeping all of this to herself, especially with her attraction to Elliot.

Lily initiated the reversal of moods by asking for something to drink, and they got up and walked over to the back window. They stood side by side gazing at the sunlit garden and woods beyond the garden. Lily stood very close, touching shoulders with Elliot and turned her eyes to meet his.

Elliot offered her coffee, a soft drink, water, orange juice, or a little white wine.

Lily said, "Oh, the wine sounds just fine...but just a little."

She followed him into the kitchen area and leaned against the island counter. He took down a couple of wine glasses, and poured the conveniently chilled wine into the glasses.

He handed Lily her glass and gently led her back to the sofa with his hand touching her back. Elliot sat in the easy chair facing her.

Lily patted the cushion beside her and asked him to sit beside her.

"If I can get things straightened out with Johnny and get Mr. Felton out of my life for good, I would like to see more of you, Elliot." Her eyes were going back and forth from the wine glass in her hand to Elliot's eyes.

It was obvious that she was flirting. Elliot knew it, but it was quite alright with him.

He had noticed her perfume the moment she came by him at the front door. He could have sworn someone had made her a special scent from the daffodils and lilac that grew near the fence at the back side of his garden.

He sat down softly beside her, so he would not disturb the drink she was holding. Lily leaned forward and placed her glass on the coaster on the coffee table in front of her.

Then, something happened that caught Elliot a bit off guard. She slid even closer and rested her head on his shoulder.

Elliot, although taken back a little, accommodated her and tilted his head so that it touched hers.

"Elliot, you're so sweet." Lily said. "I really do appreciate you helping me."

She picked up her glass and took a long, slow drink until it was completely gone. She stood up, faced Elliot, and held out her left hand toward him.

"Come and see me to the door. I have to be getting home," she said in a low, almost apologetic tone.

"Do you have to go?" Elliot replied. "We could go for a drive and maybe get some dinner."

"We had better not. At least not until we get this thing with Felton settled. I don't want him to find out that we have been talking, let alone going out together."

"He doesn't have to know anything about it. There is a brand-new restaurant called the Steak Pit on the Columbus road about fifteen miles out of town. Mr. Felton is working late at the mill tonight."

"I would love to, Elliot, but let's wait until I talk to Johnny," said Lily. "Then we can meet with him and see what happens after that. Please try to understand."

"Okay, until then. It will be tough, but until then." Elliot sighed. "And, Lily, you didn't get to see the garden. Anyway, here are some tomatoes I picked today."

He showed her to the door. He gave her a one-armed hug, and watched as she got into her car and drove away. He stood there until her car's headlights disappeared into the darkness. He flipped up his left shirt collar to again enjoy Lily's perfume, then turned to go back inside. He shut off the stoop light and closed the door.

Chapter 4

Ricky's Blunder

Lieutenant Charles Lingren put down his coffee cup next to his favorite glazed doughnuts at the Bramble Street Coffee Shop. His caseload that day was light, and it included an investigation into the fire at the school. He shook his head. *Who knew that fire could be so destructive?* he thought. He only had small pieces of evidence, and some of it was circumstantial, but he knew the key to uniting them was out there somewhere.

He became aware of some extra noise and movement to his left.

Ricky Pendleton sat down at the bar. He asked for a cup of coffee.

Mary Crenshaw brought it to him a couple of minutes later.

She slid it towards Ricky at the same time he was reaching for a napkin and his hand met the coffee causing it to splash over onto his arm.

"Ouch! You fool, what are you doing?" screamed Ricky.

The commotion caught the attention of Lieutenant Lingren.

"I'm sorry, sir," replied Mary. "It was an accident. I'll get you another cup. I bet that was hotter than the shop fire, huh?"

"What are you talking about, Mary? What has this got to do with the fire?" asked Ricky. He lowered his voice as he noticed the lieutenant sitting about ten feet away facing in the opposite direction.

"Nothin' ... nothin' ... both Ricky and the fire were pretty hot. That's all I meant," replied Mary.

Ricky finished his coffee, tossed a dollar bill on the counter and said, "Keep the change" in a sarcastic tone as he slid off his stool.

Mary said thanks and offered a receipt totaling seventy-five cents, but Ricky bolted out of the restaurant in quick fashion and did not look back.

The lieutenant heard Mary whisper to herself, "Big spender ... a twenty-five-cent tip...indeed!"

Lieutenant Lingren's curiosity was awakened not by what he overheard, but by Ricky's reaction to what seemed to be a perfectly understandable statement by the waitress. He decided he would ask her a couple of questions, when he went to the register to pay his bill.

He walked up to the counter a few minutes later, offered his money, and waited for Mary to give him his change. She handed him change for a ten-dollar bill, and the lieutenant gave her back a dollar for the tip.

He hesitated then said, "Mary, do you know anything about that shop fire? I heard you mention it, when Ricky Pendleton was in here earlier."

"Not a whole lot, Lieutenant Lingren. Ricky and Johnny Owens were in here the day after the fire, and I heard them talking about it," answered Mary. "It seemed like Ricky knew a lot about it. He was telling Johnny about how hot the flames were. I just figured he must have helped try to put it out or something like that."

"And you say that was the day after the fire?" asked the lieutenant.

"Yes, I remember because I could still smell the smoke the day they were in here." Mary said. "Kind of strange, come to think about it, though ... I couldn't hear all they said, because they started whispering. When Johnny left, he seemed very upset."

Lieutenant Lingren thanked Mary and told her that he might have more questions for her later. He asked her to call him if she could think of anything else she remembered. He went on in to the precinct and began to study what Mary had told him.

He had heard through the office scuttlebutt about Mr. Felton and Lily Owens, but had not yet realized any connection between those two and the fire he was investigating. He did, however, wonder when he saw them together, what a lovely young woman like Lily saw in such an egotistical, middle-aged, and to be quite honest, ordinary-looking man as Felton.

At least he did not make such an association until the very next day at the very same coffee shop. Again, Lieutenant Lingren was having his breakfast, when he saw Dan Felton standing outside. He looked like he was waiting on someone.

Sure enough, a couple of minutes later, Lily came up to Felton. They exchanged greetings, walked off together towards the end of the block, and disappeared around the corner.

Humm. That seems a little strange to me, thought the lieutenant. *I wonder where they are going?*

"I think I'll just see what they are up to," he muttered out loud to himself. He hustled up to the counter, paid his bill, and quickly stepped out the door. He continued down to the corner, but cautiously peeped around the edge of the building.

He saw Lily and Felton go into the vacant lot next to the saw mill. He watched as they seemed to get into an argument about something, but he was still too far away to hear what was being said.

He decided just to start walking at a normal pace towards them. He thought that maybe they would not notice him, until he got close enough to hear the gist of their conversation.

As the lieutenant got to within thirty or forty feet of the two, who were facing at an angle away from him, he heard Mr. Felton say, "You had better listen to what I am saying, Lily! You better tell your brother to keep his mouth shut about this, or I'll ..."

Felton raised his hand in anger, as the lieutenant came close enough to be noticed.

He dropped his hands quickly and turned towards him saying, "Oh, hello lieutenant. What are you doing out this way?"

"I was about to ask you the same thing, Felton. Do you have the day off or something?" queried Lieutenant Lingren.

"No, just taking a little break. I saw Lily walking by, so I came over to say, hi. That's all." squeaked Mr. Felton.

Lingren didn't let Felton know that he had caught him in a lie, but stored it away in his analytical, curious mind and told the two to have a nice day. He walked away scratching his head. He was determined that he would delve into this relationship a little further over the next few days to see if there was more to this chance meeting than was apparent.

Lily called Elliot late on a Sunday night. When Elliot answered the phone, she told him about the meeting with Mr. Felton and about Lieutenant Lingren questioning them in the vacant lot.

"What were you doing all the way over there and with Felton?" Elliot asked. "I thought you told him you didn't want to see him anymore?"

"Yes, that's right, Elliot," replied Lily. "I decided to meet him and see if Ricky might have told him anything about the fire."

"What about talking to Johnny? You told me the last time I saw you that you were going to talk to Johnny first, and then we would decide what to do next." Elliot said.

"I know, and that's what I intended to do." Lily said. "But the more I thought about it, the more I figured that I might get Mr. Felton to open up to me a little and maybe give away something that we could use to clear Johnny."

"Anyway, after the lieutenant left us alone, Felton told me that he *did* know more about the fire and that Johnny was not totally innocent. He said that Johnny and Ricky had been out at that little club on Caldera Street drinking and flirting with a couple of the girls who work there. He also told me that Ricky told Johnny that he was going to get even with the people at the machine shop. That was the night before the fire, so maybe Johnny did know about what Ricky was planning even if he didn't start the fire himself."

"It sure sounds like it. That is, if Felton is telling the truth. He might be just telling you all of that to get you to stop asking questions about things and maybe to get you back."

"Get me back?" Lily shouted. "No way ... no way in this world or the next. I wouldn't be with him if he were the last worm on earth! He might have been thinking that, but it will never happen ... never! Besides, I think now I should talk to Johnny first, then to Ricky."

"Okay, but you be careful, especially with Ricky," replied Elliot.

Lily agreed. Then, they decided to meet a few nights later on a Wednesday night at the little café that Elliot had suggested they go several days before at Elliot's house.

Chapter 5

Attempt at a Cover-up

On Monday following the meeting between Lily and Mr. Felton, Ricky was summoned to his uncle's house. Mr. Felton met him at his front door and practically yanked him into the house when he arrived.

"What did you do that for Uncle Dan?" asked Ricky.

"That fire thing is going to cause us real problems. What a knucklehead thing to do," blasted Mr. Felton. "All you had to do was to let me handle that bunch at the machine shop, but No, you had to do it your way, didn't you? Don't you see that if it gets out that you are the one who set that fire, that you will go to jail or juvenile detention? And, did you stop to realize what will happen to me? Did you? I will be ruined!"

"Well, it's too late now to do anything about it, uncle … I can't undo it, can I?" asked Ricky.

"No, but here's what you are going to do." Felton said. "You're going to go down to that shop and make doggone sure that you haven't left anything that might tie you to that fire. You wait until after midnight and go down there and look through every inch of that place. You know what you used to start the fire, so make sure none of it is still there. And I mean none of it … do you understand?"

"Yes, uncle … it was just a match but," Ricky said. "I will do it tonight."

"Make sure that you do," said Mr. Felton, "Lieutenant Lingren seemed mighty suspicious the other day when I was talking to Lily. We can't leave anything that might place to you at that site."

Ricky wasn't exactly the brightest star in the constellation, but he knew that he had better listen to his uncle or else. That same night, he dressed in dark clothes, grabbed his best flashlight, and headed down to the machine shop.

He had just about exhausted every inch of the place, when he heard noises coming from the class room door that led to the burned area. He hid behind some of the charred timbers and quickly turned off his flashlight. He saw the silhouette of a large man against the lights from the rooms behind in the school house.

He could not see who it was, but suddenly a voice boomed, "Who is out there?"

It was none other than Robert Lowry, the shop instructor. He had been in the adjacent classroom, burning the midnight oil drawing plans to rebuild the shop.

Mr. Lowry called out again. Ricky recognized the voice and stepped out into the opening. He turned the flashlight on himself. Ricky was stunned. *How in the world can I explain being in this place in the middle of the night?* He thought to himself, *I am really tired of all of this.*

"It's me … Ricky … Ricky Pendleton," he said firmly.

"Ricky? What in Sam Hill are you doing here and at this time of the night?"

Ricky had been wrestling with his conscience since the night of the fire and decided at this moment to come clean about what he had done.

"It was me, Mr. Lowry. I started the fire." Ricky said as he brought the flashlight down by his side and started sobbing. "I was so upset about the grade you gave me that I just wanted to get even with you. I know it was wrong. I'm so sorry!"

"I knew it was you, Ricky." Mr. Lowry said. "I saw you that night right after the fire started. I saw you run across the street and off into the dark. I tried to put the fire out, but by the time I called the fire department, it was too late."

"Why didn't you turn me in, Mr. Lowry?" Ricky asked.

"To be honest … I am not sure why I didn't. I guess I saw something in you that I didn't think needed to be wasted in reform school or worse yet … in prison." said Mr. Lowry. You were going to be a really fine machinist. That bad grade was intended to be a warning to you that your extracurricular activities might be getting in the way of your studies. You were actually my best student. I wanted to get your attention back on the things that mattered. Since you dropped out of school, you could be charged as an adult for arson."

"Oh, I see." replied Ricky. "I really did mess up, didn't I?"

"Yes, I guess you did, Ricky, but it isn't too late for you. You just go on home and think about things for a couple of days. There is something else that you probably did not think about when you set the fire. What about the other students? Now, they don't have a shop. We have to go down to a machine shop on the west side of town to do their work. That is more expense for the school and the parents. It brings in an element of danger when we have to go that far to finish our work. We sit inside the other building here to do class work, then wait until Saturday night to do the shop work. It is chaos, because you didn't consider the consequences. But, if you get out of this mess, you will figure a way to make things right, even if it means serving time for what you have done."

"Yes, I will do that, Mr. Lowry. Gosh, you're not so bad after all." replied Ricky. "I am so sorry for what I did."

Ricky left and went straight home, slipped in through his bedroom window, and eventually fell asleep.

Chapter 6

A Senseless Death

Lieutenant Lingren pulled up in front of the burned-out machine shop. It was separate from the main school building, but the smell of the fire still lingered in the air. He put the drab-green, unmarked police car in park and got out to look around. He walked straight over to the open side of the shop, which was blackened and wet from the rain that had begun to fall a half hour earlier.

He put on some latex gloves and covers over his shoes. He pulled out a small pen light from his jacket pocket and started looking around for anything he could find.

He had only looked for a minute, when he spotted a large shape on the floor behind one of the lathes. He tilted his head side to side and maneuvered toward it. He stopped in his tracks when he realized it was a body. He leaned down to examine it without disturbing anything. He took out his cell phone and called his office. He told the people there to get the medical examiner to the site as soon as possible along with the usual entourage of officers who needed to be there in such a situation.

He still did not know for sure who the victim was, but he soon put two and two together. It was Mr. Lowry. He bent down and gently turned the head to confirm that it was indeed him. There was still plenty of blood staining the blue denim uniform shirt that Mr. Lowry was wearing. There was more spatter on nearby burned timbers and equipment, and a deep gash in the back of his head where the blood had darkened over time. The lieutenant's initial conclusion was that this was the fatal blow.

In his investigation the day after the fire, Lieutenant Lingren had found what seemed to be pretty insignificant information, but he recorded it just in case they might later be important. The only thing not totally consumed in the fire was about one-fourth of a page from a school paper. There was no name on it, and he had no reason to believe it might help solve the case, but he was thorough and filed it away. The other piece of information was from a conversation with Mr. Lowry on that same day. Mr. Lowry had returned examination papers the day before the fire. The papers were to be returned to him within the next three days with parental signatures. The lieutenant asked Lowry to check to see who had turned in papers so far.

The fire chief had questioned Mr. Lowry as was standard operating procedure in such situations. Mr. Lowry did not offer any explanation of how the fire might have been caused, but he was pretty sure it might have started at the rag bin. He said that when he came out to try to put it out, the fire was in that area of the shop.

The lieutenant looked around until the rest of the team arrived a few minutes later and found nothing that resembled a murder weapon. *Maybe the large timber that lay beside Mr. Lowry's body just fell on him … maybe it was just an accident.*

A half hour later, the examiner's van arrived on the scene.

After the medical examiner looked over the body, he told Lieutenant Lingren bluntly, "This was no accident in my opinion. That timber has no blood on it, and the shape of it does not match the head wound. It was definitely a blunt, heavy instrument not a wooden beam. Maybe a piece of steel or something like that. I will know more when I get the body to my place and do a thorough autopsy."

The lieutenant shook his head in agreement. He continued to look around for a while. He then went over and sat in his car for a few minutes making some notes. By this time, there were onlookers everywhere. Word travels fast in the communities within a small city. In the crowd, he saw several familiar faces. One of them was Ricky Pendleton.

He wondered to himself if Ricky had been one of Mr. Lowry's students. He decided to question Ricky but wanted to get his report finished before he did so. He watched the people in the crowd, especially Ricky, as they finally dispersed and walked off in different directions. He noticed too, that there was one face missing in the crowd of onlookers. It was Mr. Felton. He worked a block from the fire, so it seemed to the lieutenant that he would be there, too. He dismissed it and went on to the office right after the medical crew left the scene with the body.

Lieutenant Lingren reasoned that he should talk to Ricky just as soon as possible. He decided to find a way to get a sample of Ricky's handwriting to compare with the only piece of physical evidence that he had found so far. That little corner of paper that somehow had not been burned in the fire was probably nothing but, after all, he was a thorough detective. But, how could he get the handwriting sample without alerting Ricky that he might be a suspect? Well, he would think of something.

Ricky made up his mind to go to the police after talking to Mr. Lowry the night before. He would do the right thing about the fire. During the long night, he reasoned that he had completely misjudged Mr. Lowry and decided it was time to quit following his uncle's orders. He was on his way to see the lieutenant, when he heard someone talking about Mr. Lowry being killed. So, that is how Ricky wound up at the police barricade. He got caught up in the flow of the crowd going that way.

As Ricky walked away, he considered that maybe he should not go to the police about the fire just yet. He would surely be the prime suspect, especially if Mr. Lowry's death was determined to be a homicide. So, he walked the seven blocks back to his parents' house on Crepe Myrtle Drive.

When Ricky walked through the doorway, his mom and dad met him just inside. His dad grabbed one arm and led him into the living room. To Ricky's surprise, there stood the lieutenant with his arms crossed. He had come directly from the crime scene.

"Ricky," said his mother. "Lt. Lungren has been waiting for you. He wants to ask you a few questions."

Mr. Pendleton started to ask Ricky what was going on, but Mrs. Pendleton quickly placed her hand over her husband's mouth and shook her head slowly from left to right to signal to stop him.

"Let the lieutenant ask his questions, dear." she muttered.

The lieutenant faced Ricky squarely and asked him to sit down.

"This won't take long, Ricky. Just covering all the bases about the death of Mr. Lowry. I have to find out everything I can from every source to find out what happened. We don't know yet if it was an accident or if there was foul play involved."

"Well, what in the world would I know about that?" interrupted Ricky almost before Lt. Lingren could finish his sentence.

"Hold on, Ricky," the lieutenant said. "I'm not saying you know anything about it at all. I just know that you were one of his students, and I am going to talk to all of you. I have to ask you where you were last night, Ricky? This is just routine, okay?"

"Sure." Ricky glanced sheepishly towards his dad and then towards his mom. "I went down to see Johnny Owens about eight o'clock, but he wasn't home, so I walked on down to get a coke at the corner market and then came on home."

"What time did you get back here?" questioned Lieutenant Lingren

"Well ... um, I guess it was about nine-thirty or so." Ricky answered.

"Does that sound about right to you Mr. and Mrs. Pendleton?" asked the lieutenant.

"I know he did leave here about eight o'clock," said Mr. Pendleton. "And he did say he was going down to see Johnny, but to be honest, I don't know exactly what time he came back. I fell asleep on the couch watching the baseball game."

"And, I'm afraid I was busy knitting," offered Mrs. Pendleton. "He could have walked right by me, and I wouldn't have noticed. I was concentrating so hard."

The lieutenant told Ricky that he would probably have to talk to him again soon after he finished with the other five students in Mr. Lowry's class. He also asked them all to give him a call at the station if they remembered anything that might help in the investigation. He left and headed back to the precinct.

Word of the homicide spread quickly through the city.

Elliot found out when Lily called him late Tuesday night. She seemed frantic, and Elliot had to calm her down to get the story out of her about what had happened.

"Lily, you say that Mr. Lowry was found in the burned down shop?" questioned Elliot.

"Yes, and you know that he and Ricky did not get along!" replied Lily.

"I know." Elliot said. "Ricky told me before the fire that Mr. Lowry gave him a bad term grade just because he was late a couple of times. I know it was more than a couple of times because some of the guys in his class told me he got there late several more times, and I saw him at the coffee shop still another time. And, you know what? Machine shop is something Ricky really liked. I think he would have been good at it too, if he had stayed with it."

Lily agreed. She said that she had to go and cut the conversation short.

"I guess we are still on for tomorrow night, then." Lily said almost as if she were out of breath. "I will meet you at your house at seven-thirty, and we will go from there."

"Okay." Elliot said. "And if you hear anything more about Mr. Lowry, let me know … and don't forget to talk to Johnny before you come to my place."

They said good-bye and both hung up their phones. Elliot sat on his couch and just sat pondering all that had happened since he met Lily. It seemed as though what he hoped would be a blossoming romance was wilting away with each new circumstance that arose. But, he would see her tonight, so he got busy with his lunch and preparing for his meeting with her.

About the same time, Ricky got back home to find that it was inquisition time with his parents.

His mom and dad pressed the issue of finding out where he had been the night before. Mrs. Pendleton had told a little fib about being busy knitting and not knowing when Ricky came home. Like any mother, she was worried any time her son was out at night. She kept listening and watching for him. She heard him when he came in around midnight.

Mr. Pendleton knew about Ricky's arrival home, as well, because his wife turned to him in bed and, with a healthy sigh, said that Ricky had come home.

Ricky insisted that he had done nothing wrong, but he could not hold up under the questioning that turned heated. His mom told him that she knew what time he came in, and Ricky crumbled under the pressure. He told her that he had gone down to the sight of the fire.

"Why would you go down there … and at that time of night?" Mrs. Pendleton asked.

"To make sure there was no evidence that could tie me to the fire, that's why! Ricky screamed. "You see, it was me … it was me. I started the fire!"

"How could you do such a thing?" yelled his dad. "So, did you also kill Mr. Lowry?"

"Dad, how could you ask such a question?" Ricky replied. "I did see Mr. Lowry there. He came out and caught me looking around, but I swear to you that I did not hurt him … I swear!"

"What happened, then. How did he die?" asked his mom at the brink of tears.

"I don't know. I told him that I was the one who started the fire." said Ricky "And you know what? He told me that he knew already that it was me. He saw me the night of the fire. I told him that I was sorry for everything, and that is all that happened."

"Well, young man … you know that we will have to go on down to the police station and talk to Lieutenant. Lingren, don't you?" insisted his dad.

"Of course! I decided to do that before I heard about what happened to Mr. Lowry. I was going to go down there this morning, but now they will think I killed him."

"I will tell you what we will do," said Mr. Pendleton. "You get some rest tonight. We'll have a good breakfast in the morning, and we will drive over there after that."

"Yes," said Ricky's Mom. "We will do that." She shook her finger at Ricky and dropped her head, as Mr. Pendleton put his arm around her shoulder and pulled her close to him.

Chapter 7

The Date

While Ricky's situation was coming to a climax on the other side of town, the time arrived for Lily to rendezvous with Elliot at his place for the dinner date/strategy session. They, of course, had no idea that part of what they were meeting about was beginning to play itself out to some extent elsewhere.

Elliot was ready, too. He had made up his mind that the things that had transpired the day before were not going to deter him from getting to know Lily much better and to simply enjoy her company. Yes, they were going to have to do some planning about Johnny's situation and how to connect the dots concerning Mr. Lowry's death, but it would be time alone with her nonetheless. Elliot still was not sure how he could help much with the investigation, but he felt that if he stood by and supported Lily, that would be something.

Lily drove up promptly at seven twenty-five p.m. and practically ran up the walkway to the front door. She rang the bell and started to ring it a second time, when Elliot opened the door. He invited her to come inside.

"Just for a minute, Elliot." Lily said. "It is good to see you, but we should get going ... we have a lot to talk about."

"I know," replied Elliot. "I will shut off all the lights in the back, and we can head on out."

It took him just a few seconds and he met Lily at the front door. He cut off the living room light and grabbed his keys off the hook near the window.

He walked towards his pickup truck. When he looked back, Lily was still heading toward her car.

He called to her, "Lily, let's take my truck tonight … pull your car to the rear of the house in case Mr. Felton happens by tonight."

"Okay." replied Lily. "Good idea."

She moved the car around and came to Elliot's truck, where he was waiting on the passenger side. He opened the door for her. She got in and thanked him for the gentlemanly gesture.

Elliot said, "You're welcome" as they backed out of the driveway and headed south towards the restaurant.

Lily was a bit more quiet and a little more distant at first than she had been at Elliot's house on their last encounter, and it prompted Elliot to ask, "What's wrong Lily … are you okay?"

"Yes, it's the murder of Mr. Lowry," she said as she began to sob. She peered out the window and continued. "I think maybe Ricky did it … to cover up the fire thing."

"Oh, did they determine it was murder, then?" Elliot asked. "The last I heard was that the police thought it might have been an accident or something. Did you hear something else today?"

Lily quickly interjected, "No … no, but it is suspicious, isn't it?"

"Yes, but let's hope that Ricky is just guilty of starting the fire and nothing else," said Elliot as he nodded for Lily to slide over closer to him.

She obliged and gave him one of those looks that could melt the Antarctic ice cap.

Elliot's heart skipped a few beats, but he managed to slowly maneuver his free arm around Lily's shoulder. There was that perfume again, just like he remembered. But, this time, he decided he had to ask her what kind it was.

Her answer only made the attraction even stronger to Elliot.

She said, "Oh, I don't wear perfume, it is probably just the late evening air … there are a lot of honeysuckles on this road this time of the year, you know."

Elliot thought to himself, *Wow! She smells like that without perfume and looks like that, too.* Then he whispered to her, “Well, I guess I will just call it Essence of Lily, then.”

Lily faked a little shyness by lowering her head and peeking up at Elliot and fluttering her long, black eyelashes at him. “I’ll bet you say that to all the girls.”

“Well, maybe to all the ones named Lily,” replied Elliot as they both broke into loud, extended laughter.

The next ten minutes passed quickly, as they drove on to the restaurant. Elliot eased the old truck into the gravel-covered parking lot. He picked out a spot in the very back corner that was not as well-lit as the rest of the lot.

He shut off the ignition, pulled up his parking brake, and went around to open the door for Lily. As she slid out of the seat and they stepped into the light, Elliot noticed for the first time that she was wearing a kind of sundress that contained every color in a field of wild flowers. She had on an azure blue shawl that looked like the sky above that field.

He held her hand to walk across the gravel. *How appropriate … Lily in a field of wild flowers adorned by the sky.*

She wore very little makeup except for the pale blue eye shadow with the least little bit of sparkles in it. The light-yellow ribbon tied her hair into a ponytail was offset to one side causing her hair to lay perfectly across her right shoulder.

The dress she wore was not bound at the waist, but fit Lily so that her exquisitely proportioned figure was more than obvious.

Elliot escorted her through the door of the restaurant.

They were greeted immediately by a hostess. "Good evening and welcome to the Steak Pit. Would you like a booth or a table?"

"Oh, the table over there." suggested Elliot.

"Oh, the one in the corner? Very romantic." replied the hostess. "Go ahead and have a seat, and the waitress will be right with you."

Elliot pulled the chair out for Lily, and he sat opposite the small, round table.

As soon as Elliot got comfortable, Lily asked, "Do you always do things like that?"

"Things like what, Lily?" he asked.

"Things like pulling the chair out and opening the car door ... that kind of thing. Are you always such a gentleman?"

"Well, guess I never really thought about it, Lily. I thought every man did those things for ladies." He replied.

"Not most of the men I know." Lily said. "In fact, I think you are the only one I know who does. And, you know what … I kind of like it … thank you Elliot."

"You deserve it, Lily, so you might as well get used to it." He replied.

Lily just smiled and reached over with her left hand, as Elliot did the same with his right hand.

The waitress arrived about the same time and greeted them. "Hello. My name is Melinda, and I will be serving you tonight. What can I get you to drink?"

Elliot asked for a wine list, but the waitress apologized and told him that the restaurant did not have a list, but that they could have either red or white wine. Elliot asked Lily if she wanted anything now. She said that she could wait until they ordered to decide. Elliot asked the waitress to just bring some water while they were waiting to order.

They both had heard that the Steak Pit served really good New York Strip, so they both ordered that with the house salad. Elliot asked for his medium well done, and Lily insisted that her steak be very well done.

Elliot ordered red wine to go with the steaks, and said to Lily as soon as the waitress walked away. "Now, Lily … haven't we had enough things burned lately?"

Lily laughed after she realized that he was referring to the shop fire, then her expression turned a little grim.

She replied, "I had almost forgotten about those awful things … for a little while, at least."

"I'm sorry, Lily, let's talk about that after we have had a great dinner," apologized Elliot.

They chatted about the weather, then the town, then Elliot's garden, and finally Lily just sighed and rested her chin on both hands in front of her. She dropped her right hand down to the table cloth, and Elliot placed his left hand on top of it.

They just sat and looked into each other's eyes for a couple of minutes.

Lily broke the silence by commenting that it was hard to tell what color Elliot's eyes were.

He said, "My mom used to tell me they were hazel. I think hazel eyes sort of look green one minute, then brown the next, I guess."

"Yes, I would call them hazel, too." replied Lily.

His comment about his mom opened the door for Elliot to tell Lily about his early life before in Eldsboro and about how his dad's accident had changed his life, etc.

Then, the waitress came with the salads and set them down. She told them that the main course would be ready in just a few minutes.

As soon as they finished the salads, the steaks arrived.

Elliot thanked the waitress and commented on how great they smelled. "I hope they taste as good as they smell!"

Lily picked up her fork and knife and started to cut into her steak, but to her surprise, Elliot raised his wine glass and offered a toast. "Lily, here's to the most beautiful girl I have ever met. May you, from this day forth, be the happiest, too."

Lily put down her knife and fork, picked up her glass, and gently touched Elliot's and toasted him. "And, to a very handsome gentleman. May you find everything that you are looking for."

They dove into the steaks and exchanged jokes and little snippets of their lives for the next half hour.

Finally, Lily said, "Well, I guess we had better talk about Johnny, Ricky, and all that other stuff. I hate to, because I am having such a wonderful time. But, I guess we should."

A storm was rolling in from the west, and they decided to talk about things on the way home. A brilliant flash of lightning startled Lily. She grabbed Elliot's arm for stability as they crossed the gravel. When they reached the truck, a few large drops of rain began to pelt the truck making a 'pinging' sound.

The thunder from the bolt rumbled across the ground ending in an echo through the nearby trees.

Elliot closed the door behind Lily and hurried to get in himself. He jumped in quickly. He slammed the door and cranked up the engine.

"Wow, that storm is coming quickly and heading straight towards town!" said Elliot.

"Yes", replied Lily. "Better take your time … it's really coming down … be careful."

Elliot eased out of the parking lot, and the rain began to come down sideways with the force of thirty mile per hour winds pushing it. He drove slowly and pulled Lily over closer to him. In fact, she had already started to slide his direction.

Elliot drove for a mile or so and told Lily that at least now they had a chance to talk a little, anyway.

The truck was swaying and being buffeted of the wind. They could hardly see where they were going. Drainage on the secondary road was not very good, and the water ponded down the sides and even across the entire roadway in places. The going was getting hazardous at best.

"There is a little side road right up there," he said as he pointed ahead and to the right. "In fact, I believe I remember a little cabin down the road a way."

"Okay, let's try it." Lily screeched. "This is a terrible storm, and I really don't like lightning at all."

Sure enough, a few hundred yards down the winding road, they saw the cabin off about fifty yards to the left side of the road. There were no lights except for one lamppost at the corner of the driveway that led up to the front door. The landscape was a bit overgrown, but had an inviting appearance, nonetheless.

Elliot pulled up near the cabin. He left the truck headlights on, so they illuminated the doorway. He flashed them several times, but no one came to the door, and no lights came on inside the cabin. There was no sign of a vehicle, and it appeared that it was either abandoned or maybe was used as a hunters' cabin during hunting season.

Elliot told Lily to wait in the truck, and he got out and ran up to the door. He knocked several times and yelled, but there was no answer.

He tried the door handle, and to his surprise, it opened. He felt inside the door frame and found a light switch. It worked! He ran back to the truck, turned off the lights and the ignition, and helped Lily up to the cabin door.

There was not much furniture in the place, only a small sitting area with a wicker sofa, a bare-bones bathroom, a tiny kitchen, and one bedroom. There was an old pot-bellied stove centered in the middle of the sitting room.

Elliot found some dry wood on the back porch, and he put several small logs in the stove along with a paper towel from his pocket. There was an old half-empty box of old matches on the stove. He lit the paper, dropped it in. In a couple of minutes, he had a beautiful fire going.

They huddled around it to dry off and sat on the sofa. They were not soaked, and they left all their clothes on to dry as they sat and talked.

"If Ricky did kill Mr. Lowry, maybe he will just turn himself in and confess to burning the shop too. That would clear Johnny, and I wouldn't have to be around that insufferable Mr. Felton ever again!"

"But what if it didn't happen that way?" Elliot asked. "What if someone else did it? Mr. Lowry may have just been out looking at the damage around the shop and something fell on his head. In fact, I prefer to think that is what happened. Ricky is certainly no choir boy, but he doesn't seem the type to actually kill someone."

"I guess you're right, Elliot, but it sure is quite a coincidence, if it was an accident after all that has happened lately. We can wait until we hear what the autopsy shows before we do anything more."

"What exactly were you thinking about doing anyway?" asked Elliot.

"I was going to confront Mr. Felton about the fire," replied Lily. "He knows it was Ricky. I was also going to tell Johnny that I am going to have to go to the police with what I know."

"You may very well be right, Lily, but there may be other things to consider. Let's wait until that report comes out, and then we can decide what to do."

He put his arm around Lily and brought his opposite hand up to her face, caressed it, and gently kissed her lips so softly that there was no sound at all. Lily responded by putting her right hand behind Elliot's head and returning the kiss with much more passion. The kiss lasted until they separated a few inches to breathe. They whispered each other's names and resumed their embrace.

Then, as if a light came on in Lily's head, she backed away and said, "Oh, Elliot, maybe we are going too fast."

"Lily, I have known you for several months now and have been falling in love with you for that long as well. It has been anything but too long for me. But, I guess, if you feel differently, we can slow down a little."

"I don't really want to," replied Lily. "I just don't want you to think I am leading you on because of my situation. This could be trouble, big trouble, and I don't want you to get hurt."

"I'm already in this up to my eyeballs, so don't even worry a minute about that. I want to help. I really do!" Elliot said. "You are very important to me, and I am not going to let you get hurt either … understood?"

Lily acknowledged with a slow nod of her head and leaned forward until her forehead rested on Elliot's chest. The storm had completely subsided by this time, and they made their way back to the truck and back towards Elliot's place. They made sure the fire was out and that everything was as they found it in the cabin.

They stood in the dark near Lily's car and had a lingering goodnight hug and kiss.

After Lily drove away, Elliot walked through his front door, closed it, and fell back against it with a satisfied sigh.

Chapter 8

The Confession

As Ricky promised, the morning after he told his parents about starting the fire, he got up and got ready to go to the police station with his mom and dad.

Mrs. Pendleton made a good breakfast, but Ricky only ate a small portion. It was obvious that he was on pins and needles about doing what he knew he had to do.

Before they left the house, his dad sat him down on the couch and said, "Son, you are doing the right thing. Whatever way this turns out, take it like a man, and your mom and I will stand by you no matter what happens, okay?"

"Yes, Dad … and I appreciate it, too," he replied. There is something else you need to know before we go. Uncle Dan has known about me burning the shop all along. I told him that Johnny was to blame for the fire. I wanted to tell someone that it was me, but he told me not to say anything to anyone else."

"Well, I'm not sure what that has to do with all that has happened, but you tell the police everything you can think of, so they don't think you had anything to do with the rest of it." insisted Mr. Pendleton.

"Yes, Dad … I promise!"

As they all arrived at the police station around nine o'clock, Lieutenant Lingren was arriving. They all went through the door. The lieutenant held the door open for them.

"Well, what brings you folks to the station? Is your cat up a tree, or something?" joked the lieutenant.

Ricky spoke up right away and said, "I'm afraid it is a lot more serious than that, Lieutenant Lingren … could we talk to you?"

"Of course. Come on down this way to my office. Would you folks like a cup of coffee and a doughnut?"

"No thank you … we just had breakfast, but you go ahead," said Mr. Pendleton. "We will wait right here for you."

After the lieutenant got back to the office with his coffee, he asked what they needed to talk to him about, plopped down in his chair, and took a long sip from his cup.

Mr. Pendleton said that he was going to let Ricky tell him.

Ricky cleared his throat and began. "Well, er, well you see, when you talked to me the morning after they found Mr. Lowry, I was afraid to say anything. But, to be honest with you, Lieutenant

Lingren… I wanted to tell you that I started that fire, but I did not kill Mr. Lowry. Honestly, I didn't. He was alive when I left that night."

"Do you mean the night of the fire?" Inquired the lieutenant.

"No, I mean the night he died," Rickey explained. "I came to the shop during the night to make sure there was nothing there that could show that I was the one who started the fire. I guess he heard me and came out and caught me looking around. We just talked. Honest, we just talked."

"Okay." asked the lieutenant. "What did you talk about, and what happened after that?"

Ricky explained that Mr. Lowry had seen him the night of the fire, and that he was willing to give him a second chance at making good in the class. Ricky told the lieutenant that he told Mr. Lowry he was sorry about the fire and that he intended to go to the police the next day.

"Well, the next day, when I started to the police station, I saw all the police cars and people standing around and found out about him being killed." Ricky said. "Then, when you came over to me, I got scared, really scared that you would think I did it. So, I decided to wait until I could get things straight in my head."

"In other words, you knew someone had killed him? Is that right?"

"Oh, no ... I didn't know what had happened," Ricky said. "But, I wasn't thinking straight, I suppose."

"It is very interesting that you should come in today and confess to setting that fire." chimed Lieutenant Lingren. "You see, I have another young man in a cell right now charged with that same crime."

"What ... who?" asked Ricky. His is parents stood up with their mouths wide open in astonishment.

"None other than Johnny Owens." replied the lieutenant. "Just when I thought things were falling into place on this, you come in here and really muddy up the waters."

"But, I'm telling the truth. It was me, but I did not kill Mr. Lowry," continued Ricky. "I was angry at him about a grade I got on a test and did a stupid, awful thing, and now he is dead. If I had not started the fire, he might still be alive!"

Mrs. Pendleton went over to her son, turned him towards her by his shoulders, and forced him to look her in the eye.

"Ricky, don't think like that. Everything is going to be alright."

Lieutenant Lingren interrupted. "Ricky, I am going to have to keep you in custody, until I get to the truth about all of this. There will be an arraignment hearing as soon as we get some things straight. In the meanwhile, Mr. Pendleton, I suggest that you get a lawyer, before we go any further. I will read Ricky his Miranda rights, but you take care of that ... he will be treated fairly here."

The lieutenant motioned for one of his officers to take Ricky back to be processed, and as he went through the large steel doors, he glanced back with tears streaming down his face.

Lieutenant Lingren consoled Mr. and Mrs. Pendleton.

Mr. Pendleton asked if Johnny had confessed also. "Did he say anything about Mr. Lowry ... about what happened to him?"

"Not exactly," the lieutenant replied. "In fact, he has hardly said a word except, 'I didn't do anything' over and over. I think he is pretty scared. It was Ricky's own uncle, Mr. Felton who now says that he knows Ricky started the fire and killed Mr. Lowry. I will keep them both in custody until we sort things out. So, folks, go on home and don't forget to contact your lawyer, and try not to worry, okay?"

As soon as the Pendletons left the station, Lieutenant Lingren made his way back to the cell where Johnny was detained.

"Johnny, guess who just came in to confess to starting the fire?" he asked.

"Who?" Johnny inquired.

"Ricky Pendleton!" replied the lieutenant. "Your good friend Ricky."

"See? I told you I didn't do anything." said a suddenly excited Johnny. "Now, can you let me out of here? Please?"

"Not just yet, young fellow. There is still the matter of Mr. Lowry's death, and by the way, the autopsy report came back today … it was murder," continued Lieutenant Lingren. "Dan Felton was convinced that you had started the fire, because Ricky told him that you did. Your parents will be here soon. I have already called them. They will have a lawyer down here soon, so be ready for all of that … he will insist on a bail hearing, but that will take a while."

And so, Johnny stayed put in the tiny cell that felt even smaller as the days went by. There was no sunlight. The cell was on the interior of the building, and sunlight was something that Johnny cherished. He longed for the time that he could get outdoors again...into the light of day and the fresh air that awaited there.

Johnny settled back on the bed in his tiny holding cell and waited for his parents to arrive. In about a half hour, they were ushered back to Johnny's cell accompanied by Lily. The lieutenant had already briefed them on the confession by Ricky, so they were encouraged about the validity of the other charge against their son.

Mrs. Owens reached through the cell bars and grabbed Johnny's hands, squeezed them, and stared into his eyes. She could sense that he was filled with a hope that was not there an hour beforehand.

"Mom ... dad ... sis, I did not kill Mr. Lowry. I swear. It must have been Ricky." Johnny blurted out. "He confessed to starting the fire ... did you hear?"

"Yes, we know," replied Mr. Owens. "Just keep cool, and I think things will get straightened out soon."

Lily walked over and put her left hand on top of his mom and brother's hands and whispered to him. "Don't you worry ... we know you didn't do it. We love, you Johnny."

The lieutenant politely asked them to say their good-byes, so they could meet with the lawyer. He had arrived and was waiting in the outer offices.

That lawyer was Ben Applegate, who had handled several homicide cases in his twenty-year career in Eldsboro and Columbus. They greeted each other, and Lieutenant Lingren offered the use of the conference room opposite his office.

Ben immediately asked if Johnny had been read his rights and asked what the specific charges were against him.

Lieutenant Lingren told him that he had been read his rights when he was taken into custody and that the charges were arson and suspicion of murder in the death of Mr. Lowry.

"On what grounds was my client arrested?" Ben asked.

"On a subpoena granted by Judge Branton on charges made by Mr. Dan Felton. He came in and told us that his nephew Ricky Pendleton had witnessed Johnny starting the fire, so we brought Johnny in this morning for questioning," said the lieutenant. "I was told by my superiors that we were to confine him until we got more information on the homicide."

Mr. Owens spoke up and told Ben that Ricky had turned himself in just a little while before they arrived and that he had confessed to the arson charge.

After a lengthy discussion on police procedures and law requirements, Lieutenant Lingren told everyone that after a thorough interrogation of Ricky, Johnny may be allowed to go home, but that it would depend also on what they could find out about Mr. Lowry's death.

Lily was pacing back and forth the whole time and seemed quite agitated. She finally shouted out, "I think you should let my brother go now … right now! Isn't it obvious that Ricky must have killed Mr. Lowry to cover up the arson?"

"That may well be the case, but we need to make sure … I am going to call Mr. Felton in today and get a lot more information from him. The charge has been made. We have to follow up … try to understand and be patient." pleaded Lieutenant Lingren.

Mr. and Mrs. Owens consoled Lily and helped her up and out of her chair. Ben nodded in agreement and shook the lieutenant's hand. He led the family out of the door, and they stopped on the front steps of the police station to talk about what they needed to do.

Ben told them that he would get all his paperwork together and call them later after meeting with Johnny later in the day.

Earlier, Lieutenant Lingren had called Mr. Felton and told him to come to the station around two o'clock that afternoon. Ben Applegate went back to his office, got his paperwork done, and came back around one o'clock to see Johnny.

Then, on into the afternoon, it was time for the meeting between Johnny and Ben Applegate in the cell block.

When Johnny saw the lawyer come through the cell block doors, he jumped up from his bed and ran to the cell door.

"Boy, am I glad to see you, Mr. Applegate. Am I getting out now?"

"Not yet, Johnny, but I assure you that I am doing everything I can do to get you out soon." Ben replied. "The lieutenant is meeting with Mr. Felton in about an hour. Maybe that will clear up things, and you can be released."

"But first," he continued, "let's you and me talk, okay?"

"Sure, Mr. Applegate, but I don't really have a lot to tell you," replied Johnny.

The jailer let Ben into the cell and they both sat on the bed. Ben got out his recorder and began to ask Johnny about what he was doing on the days and nights prior to Mr. Lowry's death.

"Well, I am satisfied that you had absolutely nothing to do with all of that, Johnny." Ben said after hearing all of Johnny's answers. "But one thing is really bothering me ... why in the world would someone like Dan Felton claim that you did it?"

Johnny sheepishly dropped his head and mumbled that he did not know why. He of course, did know. Mr. Felton had known all along that Ricky started the fire and was accusing Johnny, so that he could advance his pursuit of Lily. The hold that Dan had within the police department itself was deep, and he used his connections to get by with even more crimes against his fellow citizens than would ever come to light. Johnny eventually calmed down about getting out right away and sat back and watched what transpired next.

And, what happened next was that Dan Felton continued his assault on the truth. He was bound and determined to save face for himself, even if his own family member had to suffer for it.

Maybe because of his inherent love for his uncle, Ricky still had not mentioned that Mr. Felton knew anything about the fire or any probable involvement of his friend Johnny Owens.

He did, however, give the lieutenant a sworn statement that it was he, and he alone, who was responsible for the fire. When Lieutenant Lingren interrogated him later in the afternoon, he mentioned his uncle's name a couple of times, and that prompted the lieutenant to start zeroing in on what Mr. Felton might know about the whole matter.

Finally, Ricky gave in and filled in the facts concerning his uncle using the situation to get Lily to go out with him.

"Now, that really does open up a new can of worms, young man." asserted Lieutenant Lingren. *Now I have to ask that young lady some questions, too*. He thought.

Before that could happen, though, the lieutenant had to talk to Dan Felton.

Mr. Felton lumbered into the conference room, his brown suit rumpled and his tie slightly askew. He was perspiring heavily and declined Lingren's offer of coffee or water.

"I would prefer that we get on with this, if you don't mind, lieutenant." he said anxiously. "I've got better things to do than hang around here all day, you know?"

"Well, first of all, you need to know that your nephew Ricky came in a couple of hours ago and confessed to setting the shop fire." returned the lieutenant forcefully.

"He did what?" shouted Felton. "I told him to ..." He caught himself in the middle of saying something that he shouldn't say and stopped in mid-sentence. "I mean, I told him that Johnny was to blame for all of that."

"What was it you almost said, Felton? Maybe that you told Ricky not to say anything at all, perhaps?" asked Lieutenant Lingren.

"No, of course not, and I don't like the tone in your voice!" Felton said, "I told him not to say anything about something he knew nothing about ... that's all. And furthermore, if you are implying that I had anything to do with all of this, you had better get your facts straight, mister."

"Hold on there, Felton. I didn't intend to imply anything of the sort." snapped Lieutenant Lingren, "but I will ask whatever questions I need to in order to solve this case ... understand?"

"Yes, I do ... sorry if I got a little out of line with you lieutenant." Felton replied. "Go right ahead with your questions ... I am here to help."

"That's better. Now, where was I? Oh yes, since Ricky confessed to the arson, I need to understand what gave you the notion that Johnny started the fire."

"Well, right after the fire happened, Ricky told me that Johnny was the one who started it." said Mr. Felton.

"Could it be that he lied to you about the whole deal ... including the murder?" asked the lieutenant.

"No, no, no!" replied Felton. He couldn't actually hurt anyone. He is basically a good young man. I'm sure he had nothing to do with the murder ... it was murder, wasn't it lieutenant?"

"Yes, indeed ... the coroner's report is quite clear about that. Mr. Lowry was struck not once but three times in the head with a heavy metal object. The first blow probably killed him, and apparently the killer wanted to make sure he was dead."

"I need to ask you about Lily … Lily Owens. I understand that you have been seeing her socially; is that right?" asked the lieutenant.

"Yes, but I don't see what that has to do with this case. Besides, we have not been out in a while now." replied Mr. Felton. "We had a disagreement, and we decided not to see each other for a while."

"Well, I know. I accidentally overheard you two arguing a week or so ago out near the site of the fire," quipped Lieutenant Lingren. "It sounded like you were the one who was angry … you were saying something about her brother keeping his mouth shut. What exactly were you talking about, Felton?"

"Nothing to do with this." snapped Mr. Felton. "Nothing at all to do with this … I assure you!"

"According to Ricky, you knew that he had started the fire. Did you tell Ricky to blame this on Johnny Owens, so you could gain an advantage with Lily?" asked the lieutenant in a bold, business-like tone.

"Most certainly not … and if you have some charge to make against me, I suggest you go ahead and make it. I will just quit talking to you right this minute. I will talk to my lawyer, so you charge me with something, or I'll be on my way." said Mr. Felton.

"Okay, you go ahead with your lawyer. I'll call you when I need you again." Lieutenant Lingren retorted.

Felton did a quick about-face and stormed through the doorway.

Lieutenant Lingren wondered why he didn't even ask to see his nephew. His suspicions grew in regard to Felton's possible involvement. Now, he set out to contact Lily to see how her version of things coincided with Mr. Felton's.

Chapter 9

Felton's Folly

Lily Owens spent the next day at home. She told her parents that she did not feel like going anywhere, especially to work. She was obviously depressed about Johnny, but she could not bring herself to go down to the police station to see him.

Instead, she kept to herself in the comparative safety of her room.

Late in the afternoon, her father got a call from the police department. They asked him to have Lily come down the next morning at ten o'clock to talk to Lieutenant Lingren. He went up to her room a few minutes before three o'clock to tell her and found her sitting by an open window crying.

He put his hand on her shoulder, and she looked up into his eyes. She stood up facing him directly. He placed his hands, first one then the other on her shoulders and asked her what was wrong.

She told him that she was worried about Johnny even though she knew the charges against him would be dropped soon. She told her dad that Johnny being arrested could have been avoided, if she had come forth about Mr. Felton and what she knew about Ricky's involvement.

Her dad consoled her and told her that he and her mom would go with her the next day to the police station and for her not to worry. It would be over soon.

Lily calmed down or at least she appeared to do so for her father's benefit. She promised to try to rest, and as soon as he left, she called her boss and explained to him that she would come to work as soon as she finished with Lieutenant Lingren.

The next phone call she made was to Elliot. When Elliot answered, she told him all that had happened since she had last seen him. Elliot offered to go to the police station with her, but she said that she didn't think it would be a good idea and that her parents would be with her.

They agreed to meet right after Lily got off work at Elliot's house the next evening.

Lily and her parents arrived promptly the next morning at the station, and Lieutenant Lingren asked Mr. and Mrs. Owens to wait in the lobby area, while he questioned Lily. He assured them that this was merely a routine session and that she could have a lawyer present if she wanted.

Lily said, "I don't need a lawyer … let's go ahead. I want my brother out of here as soon as possible."

The lieutenant told Mr. and Mrs. Owens they could visit with Johnny if they wished, and they obliged.

As soon as they got into the room, Lieutenant Lingren asked Lily directly about her relationship with Mr. Felton, and she gave pretty much the same story as Felton had earlier.

"Now then, Miss Owens, I need to know everything you can tell me about what you know about the fire at the school shop, and I mean everything! Don't leave out a single detail. All of this, I am sure," continued the lieutenant, "is tied into the murder of Mr. Lowry, and so it means that someone committed that awful act and could get the ultimate punishment … death or life in prison."

"Yes, I am fully aware of that." Lily said. "I will tell you all I can. I know that Mr. Felton knew that Ricky started the fire. Johnny told me that Mr. Felton would accuse him, if I did not go out with him. Felton said it would be big trouble for Johnny, so I went along with it for a while."

"And then?" asked Lieutenant Lingren. "What then?"

"Well, when you saw us arguing that day, when you talked to us over near the school …

he threatened me and told me that Johnny had better keep his mouth shut about the fire. That's when you came up, but he finished what he was saying after you left. He said that he was going to turn Johnny into the police."

She continued, "So, I told him that I was tired of being bullied by him. I went directly to Johnny and told him what Felton had said to me. Johnny told me that he was not afraid of him and not to worry."

The lieutenant had recorded the entire session and told Lily that she could go, and they went out to the lobby. He gave Lily's parents a short version of what Lily had told him. Mr. Owens asked the lieutenant what was going to happen next. He told them that he would have to talk to everyone again with this new information in front of him and that he would let them all know when he had more to tell them.

And so, after all the investigations were completed to the satisfaction of the lieutenant and his supervisors, Ricky was arraigned and charged with arson and first-degree murder. He had just turned eighteen years of age a few months earlier, and he would be tried as an adult.

Johnny Owens was released the morning after the confession by Ricky to the arson charge.

Lieutenant Lingren visited all the people involved at least one more time and was convinced that Ricky was indeed the right person to be awaiting trial. The trial was set for three weeks from this date.

Lily and Elliot saw each other at least two or three times each week and drew closer with each passing day. The pressure was off the couple with Johnny's release, and their association with Dan could now become distant.

At work, Elliot finally settled into his role and happily avoided Mr. Felton, who seldom spoke to him even in the occasional business meeting that threw them together in the same room.

It turned out to be a relatively short-lived break in their hostilities, however. One day, right after he arrived at work, Elliot's immediate supervisor, Frank Miller came into his office. Frank greeted Elliot with a wry smile, slapped a manila envelope down in front of Elliot, and sat in the straight back chair facing Elliot's desk.

"What's this, Mr. Miller?" asked Elliot.

"It is a summons for you to appear at a company ethics meeting tomorrow." replied Mr.

Miller. "It seems that Mr. Felton has made some serious accusations against you. He says that you altered inventory reports and caused him to lose bonuses that he should have received."

"But, Mr. Miller, I swear to you that I did no such thing!" asserted Elliot. "He is just jealous of Lily Owens and me … he thinks I stole her away from him."

"No need to cry on my shoulder, Elliot. I am not the one you need to convince. Get your ducks in a row, get copies of all of your records, and be at that meeting at four o'clock tomorrow afternoon." instructed Mr. Miller.

"I'm sorry, Mr. Miller. I didn't mean to snap at you. You're right. I will be ready." Elliot said.

After Mr. Miller left, Elliot began to gather up what might be needed. The more he thought as he worked, the more he wondered *what Felton that could possibly have that could prove any wrongdoing. All I can do is to be sure I have the records from that work period and to hope for the best.*

When he got home, he called Lily right away to let her know about the inquiry. She didn't seem surprised at all and told him that she would come over, if he wanted her to help him get ready. He thanked her, but he said that he would be better off just studying his documents and thinking about what he might say to defend himself. He didn't tell her as much, but he thought she would be a distraction. They had become very close, and any meeting between the two might have romantic overtones that would cause him to lose focus on the tasks that lay before him.

And, that is how the rest of the evening went. Elliot organized the production logs and printed out all other notes he could find that might be useful at the meeting. He also remembered the video cameras he had installed at the gates. He had copies of those tapes made earlier in the day and stowed them away in his briefcase. He was as prepared as he could be.

When he walked into the waiting room outside the conference room the next day just before four o'clock, he sat with his briefcase on his lap, until the receptionist received a 'buzz' to have him come into the room.

Mr. Miller was already there and pointed to the seat at the end of the large oval table, where he was to sit. Mr. Felton was there, too at the opposite end of the table.

The chief financial officer, Mr. Oxendine was to Elliot's left, and the other company officials were on the other side of him.

Mr. Oxendine called the meeting to order and immediately noted that everything said was being recorded.

He then pointed to Mr. Felton and read the charges he had made from the documents in front of him.

Then he looked over to Elliot and said, "Elliot Timberlake, I am going to ask you directly to begin with. Did you, in fact, alter the production records for April 1 through June 30, 2012?"

Elliot replied, "No sir. I absolutely did not. I have all my records for the past several months in my briefcase. They show individual deliveries and all the numbers for the various processes such as debarking, treating, trimming, etc. I have the logs from each of those departments here with me as well."

Mr. Oxendine nodded with approval at Elliot's order and apparent confidence in his opening remarks. He then said to Mr. Felton, "Okay. Mr. Felton, let's get on with this. You have charged this young man with serious and career-threatening allegations. You have given us log sheets that show tallies you say are much lower than they should be for the period of work in question."

Elliot, let's compare your log with the numbers Mr. Felton has submitted to us. What do your records show for the months of April through June?

Elliot ran his fingers down his ledger until he reached those dates and said firmly, "We had eighty-eight trucks come in during that period of which we processed all but one cord off the last truck."

Mr. Oxendine pointed out that Mr. Felton's report showed ninety-one trucks being unloaded for the same period of time.

Mr. Felton interrupted and said in a stern but shaky voice, "That's quite a difference, isn't it ... it cost me my bonus for all three months, and it didn't stop there either."

"Wait a minute, Felton." ordered Mr. Oxendine. "Let's look at this a little closer. Why weren't the extra trucks processed?"

"I'll tell you why, because the ledger was changed ... that's why," shouted Mr. Felton.

Mr. Oxendine looked over the pages of Elliot's log and compared them with Mr. Felton's side by side in front of him.

"Elliot," he said. "You say that eighty-eight trucks came in. You unloaded the logs, they were debarked, and all of those went on to be treated and planked … is that right?"

"Yes sir." Elliot replied. "All were debarked except that one chord that we held back, because we found red heart disease in them. They should not have been harvested in the first place. They are still laying out in the reject yard, if you would like to see? They are labeled with the lot number and date".

"Yes, we will look at that in just a little while." said Mr. Oxendine. "Elliot, do you have any explanation for the three missing loads that Mr. Felton claims came in during those three months?"

"No, but I have my suspicions …"

Elliot was interrupted by Mr. Felton's hysteric "What do you mean, you little upstart? Are you accusing me of something?"

Mr. Oxendine calmed down he two men and reminded them that they were in the middle of an inquiry and that they would both confine their remarks to the questions asked.

"Now, Elliot, I want you to tell us about your suspicion. I will give you a few minutes to produce any evidence you may have to support your case." directed Mr. Oxendine.

Elliot took a deep breath and said that he had been threatened by Mr. Felton on several occasions, because of his relationship with Lily Owens. As he explained the relationship in detail, Mr. Felton's face turned every shade of red found in a large box of Crayola crayons. He said that his only evidence about what had been processed in the months in question were his official records, his signed testimony of his three workers, and one other item that he would present later. He handed his documents to Mr. Oxendine, avoided eye contact with Mr. Felton, and returned to his seat.

When Mr. Oxendine finished looking over the documents Elliot had given him, he passed them down the line to the other company officials, including Mr. Miller. They took turns browsing through the data, and when all were finished, passed the pages back to Mr. Oxendine.

Before he could tell anyone what was going to happen next, Mr. Felton exploded again shouting, "You can't go by any of that baloney … they are all plotting against me!"

"Now, now, Felton, settle down." directed Mr. Oxendine. "We'll decide what is baloney and what is truth. Right now, we are all going out to the reject pile and inspect those logs that Mr. Timberlake says are there. Until then, you will both remain quiet, or I will ask that you both be removed from this plant by security ... understood?"

They both shook their head in agreement, and the group left the office area and meandered through the plant and out to the lumber yard.

Mr. Oxendine asked Elliot to point out where the logs in question were. He did so, and each member of the examination team filed past and looked at the labels, which all showed dates between early April and late May. Each tag also showed in big, red letters, "Do not use ... Red Heart Disease."

Mr. Felton held his peace, although he was fit to be tied. He saw the labels, also.

The meeting reconvened in the conference room, and Mr. Oxendine told everyone to settle down. He then asked Mr. Felton to present his case.

"First, those labels don't mean anything either. They could have been put on the logs yesterday, for all we know. Secondly," Felton said. "I always count the number of trucks coming through the gate, so that I can figure my bonus at the end of the month, and there were ninety-one trucks that came through those gates ... not eighty-eight. And, something else, I don't know what Elliot is talking about in reference to Lily ... that's just a fabrication. I am old enough to be her father, and besides, that is my business."

"Okay, okay." cautioned Mr. Oxendine. "Hold on a minute. It is easy enough to corroborate Elliot's story about the young lady, but I have some bad news for you, Mr. Felton. You see, I recognized those labels. They are the design we used up until guess when? June first, 2012. After that, we started using the diamond shape, so the ones we saw had to be put on before June first."

Mr. Felton's jaw dropped.

Elliot looked surprised. He had forgotten that they were indeed the new labels.

Mr. Oxendine asked, "Elliot, how is your count done ... manual or otherwise?"

"I do it manually, Mr. Oxendine, but there is a sure-fire way to check against my numbers ... if you will allow me?"

"By all means, go ahead young man. This is getting more interesting by the minute." directed Mr. Oxendine.

Elliot opened his briefcase and pulled out a video tape. He got up from his chair and inserted it into the machine on the table. He told everyone that he had installed a camera at the entrance to the plant two weeks after he was promoted to his supervisory position. He pointed to Mr. Miller and said that his supervisor had given him permission to do so. Mr. Miller nodded yes, and Elliot pushed the button and ran the video.

Mr. Felton stood up and yelled, "What kind of trickery is this?"

Elliot noted, as the video progressed that the date and the time were at the bottom right of the screen. "If you will count as the trucks come in, you will total eighty-eight and no more."

At the end of the tape, the officers leaned in, whispered to each other for a few minutes, and shook their heads in agreement. Then Mr. Oxendine sat up straight in his chair and stated, "There are exactly eighty-eight trucks coming through that gate ... not ninety-one. We will have the tape examined to see if it has been altered, but I can tell you, Mr. Felton, it looks like to us that Elliot is right about the number of trucks coming in and about the rejects in that lumber yard.

We will adjourn the meeting at this point and recall everyone tomorrow to announce our findings. Until then, you are to have no contact with one another. We will meet promptly at four o'clock here.

At the meeting the next day, Mr. Oxendine called everyone to order, and in a very matter-of-fact manner stated, "Our inquiry is complete. Mr. Felton, we find no substantiation to your allegation that Mr. Timberlake did anything wrong. We do not see any evidence that he altered any logs or ledgers. We furthermore believe that you acted out of malice towards him because of personal reasons in bringing forth those allegations."

"As a result, we will allow Mr. Timberlake to leave this proceeding and to continue his work with our sincere apologies for having put him through this process. You may leave now, Mr. Timberlake, unless you have any comments."

"Yes, I would like to say something," Elliot said as he turned to face Mr. Felton. "I just want you to know that I don't harbor any ill feelings toward you. I hope we can put this all behind us."

He offered his hand.

Mr. Felton just lowered his head without shaking Elliot's hand.

Elliot thanked the committee and slowly turned and walked through the door.

He wanted very much to let his emotions explode onto Mr. Felton in front of the whole company leadership, but his innate and very mature nature kept him from doing so.

Mr. Oxendine stood, scratched his head and came around the conference table to a position near Mr. Felton.

He said, "Felton, we have discussed possible punishment for what you tried to do. We have decided to put you on probation in your job. We are going to let you continue as long as you do not let this sort of thing happen again."

You have been a loyal employee for many years. We feel that you have earned this consideration, but by no means are we condoning what you tried to do to that young man."

And so, without saying anything further, Mr. Felton left and did concentrate on his work for many months after that day. He made no contact with Lily and refused to even go by to see his nephew Ricky who was awaiting trial for the burning of the high school shop and the murder of Mr. Lowry.

Chapter 10

The Trial

Ricky Pendleton was arraigned and held over for trial, and Ben Applegate, who had earlier represented Johnny Owens, took over as Ricky's defense attorney.

He had stated to the District Attorney weeks before that he thought there was a good chance Ricky was not guilty of murder-that something just did not seem right. He had a feeling there was something missing from the story.

The trial was set for late August, four months after the murder. In that time, Mr. Applegate had amassed very little in the way of proof that Ricky was innocent. He had circumstantial things like Mr. Felton's instructions to Ricky to go to the site that night to make sure that there was no evidence to point toward Ricky setting the fire. All of that was of little consequence in corroborating Ricky's claim that he did not kill Mr. Lowry.

However, Mr. Applegate could not get out of his mind that if Ricky had remained quiet about starting the fire and had indeed killed Lowry, he could not have been placed at the scene of the crime that night.

Mr. Applegate left no stone unturned, he thought, but came up completely empty on anything that might clear Ricky. He explained to Ricky that he needed something, some starting place or a clue of some sort that would lead to new evidence which could clear him. Sadly, though, he had to tell him that, if no such evidence came to light, there wasn't much that could keep him from being convicted of both the arson and the murder charges.

The only other person, according to Ricky, who knew he was going to the fire scene the night of the murder was his uncle, Dan Felton.

Ben talked to Dan several times before the trial and pleaded with him to tell him anything that might help Ricky to no avail.

Ben finally admitted to himself that Felton was a dry well, but he maintained a feeling that he knew something. He believed Ricky's statement that his uncle had pushed him to go to the shop area that night to look for evidence that might implicate him in the arson case.

But, at the trial, Mr. Felton provided an airtight alibi, a date that he claimed to have that night with a woman who testified she had been with Felton until three o'clock in the morning on the night of the murder.

The prosecution had plenty of circumstantial evidence and facts placing Ricky at the scene at around the time the coroner determined was the time of death, and he had a motive.

The jury took only an hour to return their verdict of first-degree murder. They did not recommend the death penalty, and the judge sentenced Ricky to life imprisonment at the state penitentiary in Columbus.

Ricky was transferred there three days later. He insisted at every opportunity that he was innocent, and his lawyer promised to appeal the conviction and ask for a new trial as soon as possible. Ricky would be eligible for parole in twenty-five years. He felt in his heart that he deserved to serve some time for starting the fire, but he hoped that Mr. Applegate could reopen his case one day. He often thought that he stayed loyal to Johnny and Lily by never divulging the blackmail by his own uncle.

He thought that might have been a mistake, but deep down, he just could not believe his uncle could actually kill anyone. Maybe a thief had seen them, waited for Ricky to leave, and seized the opportunity to rob and kill Mr. Lowry. He offered that theory to his lawyer, and

Ben proposed that to the police department. It turned out that Mr. Lowry's wallet with over one hundred dollars in it was still on the body the next morning, so the robbery possibility was erased.

Ricky remained silent about those things, and the days turned into weeks, the weeks turned into months in prison. His hope soon began to fade.

Johnny came to see Ricky about once a week for the first few months, and then his visits became less frequent due to his new job at a paper mill in Lancaster, Ohio. His hours were long, and he often worked seven days a week, so there was little time to do anything else but work.

When Johnny did come, there was little to talk about other than what had happened the night of the murder and, of course, asking about their families, etc. They talked about Eldsboro and Johnny's work and always finished the visit with conversation about how Johnny could help find new evidence that might help him get a new trial. Johnny told Ricky that Lily's boyfriend, Elliot, was poking around and trying to help him find anything that might help clear him. He said that he had asked him to help as a favor to him, because he never believed that Ricky could kill anyone.

There was little that Johnny could do besides listen to all the details Ricky could remember about the night of the murder. Johnny kept insisting that what happened after he talked to Mr. Lowry earlier in the night could provide him an alibi. It did not help matters at all that Ricky insisted that he simply went home that night and went straight to bed without anyone seeing or talking to him.

Lily and Elliot talked about Ricky and the relationship between Ricky and Johnny many times. In their earlier questioning in regard to the murder of Mr. Lowry, they said as little as they could about that friendship, so their secret remained a secret. They both knew about the covenant they had made in order to keep Mr. Felton at bay and feared what he might do to them, if they ever told of his blackmail.

Besides, they had their own lives to live. Elliot's work at the mill turned into a lucrative career, and as time moved on, so did Elliot and Johnny.

Chapter 11

A Blossoming Romance

Elliot was a romantic at heart, but his shyness slowed his approach to Lily to a snail's pace. He decided months ago that he was going to propose to Lily. He wanted to plan the proposal, so that it would be something she (and they) would remember for the rest of their lives, a moment to remember throughout their lives together, and hopefully for their children and grandchildren.

It was mid-winter, and he thought maybe the best time to ask her would be Valentine's Day, until he remembered he had promised his mom that he would visit her that entire week.

He asked himself. *What about spring? Yes, that's it! I will propose to her at the same place where we met … in my garden. Yes, when all the crops and flowers are in full blossom.*

Over the next few days he formulated his plans and worked out the details in his mind. It would be at least three more months before the garden would be pretty enough (in his mind's eye) to make it just right. He reckoned that he would work extra hard through the rest of the winter and into planting season to make sure it was just right.

He decided to plant sunflowers around the entire perimeter of the field to accent everything else he wanted to plant. He was sure that he would have corn, beans, peas, tomatoes, some melons and cantaloupes, and he also decided to alternate every other row with flowers. He decided to plant daffodils, snapdragons, daisies, and gladiolas; *yes, lots of gladiolas.*

Elliot and Lily had a standing date for Tuesdays, Fridays, and Saturdays. They did all the usual things that young people like to do on dates. They went to the movies, carnivals, days out on the lake, and just driving through the countryside. They often went back to the Steak Pit for dinner on the weekends, and it became their favorite restaurant.

There was a juke box in the far corner, and they loved to dance a lot, mostly doing their own style of waltz and slow dances to any music with a beat that suited their mood.

After Elliot returned from his mother's house in mid-February, he took Lily back to the restaurant, and every song played that night was danceable music. Elliot held her close, their faces touching lightly. He twirled her and pulled her back to his embrace. As the last notes of the last song played, he kissed her gently and walked her back to the table.

"Would you like some coffee or dessert, Lily?"

"No thank you, Elliot ... I just had my dessert." She replied. "Why don't we just drive back to your house and take our time getting there? I have enjoyed tonight so much, and I don't want it to end just yet."

"You read my mind, sweetheart." Elliot whispered. "Let's do that ... no hurry at all."

"Elliot, that's the first time you ever called me anything but Lily. It sounded very nice, very nice indeed."

He got up from his chair, went around to hers, pulled it back, and held her hand as they left to go to his truck parked outside. Yes, he still drove a truck, but now he had a new one. He still used his old one for hauling and other farm chores, but he used the new one for dates with Lily.

Lily slid over close to Elliot, as he started out of the parking lot. He put his arm snuggly around her shoulders. Lily wiggled a little to make sure that every part of her that could conform to every available space on Elliot's right side did so.

The ride back to town was smooth, and they reminisced about their relationship and the things that had happened since they met.

Lily stretched her neck up and kissed Elliot's face.

He smiled and looked over at her with a slight giggle and asked, "What was that for?"

"Just because," she replied. Just because I think you are the best, and I love you so much."

"I love you too, Lily," he said as they both became so quiet that the only sound was the roar of the new truck's engine and an occasional thumping sound from bumps in the pavement.

When they arrived at Elliot's house, he kept his arm around her all the way up to the front door. They paused and stared into each other's eyes for a moment, and they slowly came together for what may have been a kiss of the covenant that was soon to come.

However, Elliot's proposal was still months away. He could hardly keep himself from asking her when they sat down on the sofa, but his resolve was to wait until the spring. He had originally wanted to propose on Valentine's Day, but the idea of doing that with all the flowers changed his mind. He did, however hint around that such a question by him was in the offing.

"Lily, how do you like my place here … I mean could you be happy here?" Elliot prodded. "You know that I am saving up for a real ranch. I have already been looking at a couple of places. One is about one hundred acres and the other is one hundred and forty acres. They are both hilly and both have barns. One has a nice farmhouse; the other needs a lot of work. I thought I would have some cattle, a few horses, chickens, and an even bigger vegetable garden than I have now."

"That sounds wonderful, Elliot." Lily replied. "I think your place here is great, too. It is quaint. The house is a little small, but with a little tender loving care, it could be a neat cottage … don't you think?"

"Well, sure, but I have always wanted lots of space." Elliot continued. "We wouldn't … er, I mean I wouldn't be so far from town, but there would be plenty of land to stretch my wings, you know?"

"I know. I think either place would be grand." Lily said. "That reminds me. I wanted to ask you if you would come over to our house for

Thanksgiving dinner? It will be you, me, Johnny, mom and dad. What do you say, Elliot?"

"I don't know Lily." I have a lot to do here … it will be harvest time and all. Let me think about it, and I will let you know."

"Please, Elliot." Lily begged. "My parents really like you, and Johnny does, too. You'll enjoy it. Lily looked into his eyes with one of those looks that no man can resist. "Please".

"Okay then. Sure, I will come, but under one condition." Elliot replied. "You must let me supply all the vegetables for the meal. I will have plenty of corn, beans and peas, and the pumpkins look like they are going to be the best this year that I have ever grown."

"I'm sure that will be more than alright with Mom." she assured Elliot.

"So, go ahead and ask them if it will be alright for me to come." he said.

"I already have, my Love." Lily replied with another one of those looks. "Then, it's all set."

In the back of Elliot's mind, he had been thinking all this time that he needed to get to know Lily's family better, especially if he was going to propose marriage to her soon. In fact, this would be a perfect setting to ask her father for Lily's hand in marriage. Yes, it was a bit old-fashioned, but Elliot was that way. He never really got both feet into the twentieth century, let alone the twenty-first. He loved reading about the way things were when chivalry was the norm. He told himself that treating others with respect was the only sure way that he could expect to receive the same in return.

They sat and talked for a while. They kissed good night at the doorway, and Elliot walked Lily back to her car. She threw him a kiss as she backed out of the driveway, and he waved a slow good-bye.

As the summer ended, and the autumn became a glorious display of nature's palette of colors, Elliot worked tirelessly on harvesting all the bounty from the garden. Some things like the vegetables had to be picked right away and stored for later consumption. He set aside plenty of those things for the Thanksgiving feast.

The pumpkins were a bit later in ripening and seemed to relish the cooler air. He harvested a few for decoration around Halloween and to donate to local churches for fundraising and saved a few for Thanksgiving. One, in particular was a large, almost perfectly round specimen that probably weighed sixty pounds or more. It remained firm and kept growing right up to the week before Thanksgiving along with a couple of smaller ones that would be great for pies, etc.

In the days that followed, Lily was quite busy, too. Seasonal work had picked up and when she was not at work, there was plenty to do in preparation for the long holiday season just ahead. There was shopping, lots of shopping for Christmas to do. She liked to get that done before the first of December, so she could take full advantage of Black Friday deals in Eldsboro. She also made trips to Columbus for her high-end gifts.

Her thoughts, when not on those things and Elliot, drifted back to Ricky and even to Mr. Felton. She did not want to think of all of that, but she never really considered Ricky as someone who would actually kill someone. Those thoughts were just flashes that came on suddenly and left suddenly, because there was so much to do.

Johnny was constantly reminded about Ricky by Mr. Felton, who made it a point to needle him about his nephew's fate whenever he could. Felton's feelings for Lily had not changed, as she turned her full attention to Elliot, and he would often ride by Elliot's farm to see if Lily was there. He would park down the highway and sometimes follow them and show up where they were, pretending to be there purely by coincidence.

One day, the week before Thanksgiving, Felton happened to show up at the diner near the school to have lunch. Of course, Elliot and Lily were there having a sandwich. Felton sat at a table near them. They exchanged tenuous greetings, and Mr. Felton ordered a BLT and a glass of iced tea. While he waited, he stared relentlessly at Elliot who was facing him.

Lily's back was to Felton, but she knew his tactics and noticed that Elliot was quite uncomfortable.

"Elliot, let's get out of here … I've lost my appetite. Let's go."

"Sure, Lily. It's kind of cold in here, if you know what I mean." Elliot replied.

They left quickly. Elliot looked back over his shoulder at Mr. Felton, who continued his stare until they got completely out of the door.

Elliot assured Lily. "Don't worry about that crazy man. If he keeps harassing us, I will go to the police and get a restraining order against him."

Lily nodded and they walked on down the block to Elliot's truck. As they passed in front of the diner, they saw Mr. Felton standing at the window watching them go by.

They didn't let that incident bother them too much, and Thanksgiving Day came. Lily's mom had prepared a great feast including lots of things from Elliot's garden. She baked things like pies from the pumpkins he brought to her a few days before. The large pumpkin that he brought was on proud display on the front door stoop and greeted Elliot as he arrived for dinner. He smiled when he saw it and rang the doorbell.

Mr. Owens answered the door and invited him to come and sit on the couch in the den. They talked for a few minutes, and Lily came down the stairs. Elliot stood and smiled broadly. She came over to him and hugged him. Johnny came in from the kitchen along with his mom.

They exchanged pleasantries, and Mrs. Owens said, "Dinner is ready ... let's go into the dining room."

Lily sat next to Elliot at the large rectangular table. Mr. Owens was at the head of the table and his wife was at the opposite end. Johnny sat directly opposite Lily.

Mr. Owens prayed. "Father, we thank you for the bounty of the season, for the skilled hands that grew and provided the food, and for the loving hands that prepared it. Let it all be nourishment for our bodies and may your grace be nourishment for our souls. In Your Holy name … Amen."

The giant roast turkey, garnished with vegetables from Elliot's garden was surrounded by dressing and was the centerpiece of the table. Cranberry sauce, beans, peas, corn, homemade bread, and rice were passed around to fill every plate.

"Wow! What a spread!" Elliot said. "You really know how to do the fixings, Mrs. Owens."

"Thank you, Elliot, but I can't take all the credit. Lily helped me with the cooking, and my dear husband carved that magnificent bird."

"And what about me?" Johnny blurted out. "I did most of the leg work … back and forth to the market and helping Elliot bring all of his stuff."

"Yes." Everyone responded in unison and all erupted in mock applause.

Johnny giggled and said, "Pass me the cranberry sauce, please."

Everything was delicious, and the the pumpkin pie for desert was a perfect ending to a perfect meal.

Mr. Owens and Elliot excused themselves and went out the back door to the patio. Johnny went back to his room for an after-dinner nap.

Elliot cleared his throat a couple of times and tried to speak. He finally had to be prodded by Mr. Owens. "Elliot, what's on your mind? What is it you want to say … go ahead."

It was as if Lily's father knew what was coming.

"Well, it's like this, Mr. Owens … I mean, you see I am in love with Lily … your daughter. I have been in love with her since I first saw her I think, and I … I would like to ask for your permission to ask her to marry us … er … I mean me."

"Does Lily know you are ready to ask her?" asked Mr. Owens. "Did she know that you were going talk to me about this today?"

"No, and please don't tell her that I asked you … whether you say it is okay or not." replied Elliot. "I want it to be a surprise."

"No problem, Elliot, but my answer is that you do have my permission." responded Mr. Owens. "But when are you going to ask her?"

"I want to ask her in the spring. I've got it all planned out." Elliot said.

Mr. Owens told Elliot that he thought it would be hard to wait that long, but that it would give them both time to make sure about everything.

Elliot agreed and promised that he would be a good husband and would protect Lily no matter what.

As he drove home later, Elliot purposed in his heart that he would rededicate himself to his work. He decided that he needed to do that for Lily's sake and for the sake of the future he they would have together.

He again kicked the bar exam down the road until he and Lily were on a firmer foundation. He and Lily would talk more about that in the coming days as they set in motion the plans for their wedding.

Chapter 12

Twists and Turns

So, as good things were happening for Lily and Elliot, Ricky was mired in a deep depression in his prison cell. He had few visitors except for Johnny Owens, who remained loyal and came when he could. Mr. Felton came less and less often as the weeks went by, but Ricky did not mind him not being there very much. As time passed, he realized his uncle had indeed led him down many wrong paths.

His lawyer, Ben Applegate called every two weeks or so to him an update on any progress he had made on an appeal for a new trial. Most calls were negative, because there was no new evidence that would make a new trial possible.

There was, however, someone who did come to see Ricky on a regular basis. It was Mary Crenshaw, the waitress from the diner. She and Ricky had been seeing each other secretly for more than a year before the murder of Mr. Lowry. She was fifteen years older than Ricky, so they had clandestine meetings when they could over that entire time period. Ricky reasoned that if anyone knew about his relationship with Mary, she would become the brunt of all sorts of persecution from the town and their families, especially Mr. Felton. Ricky already knew first-hand what his uncle could do with that kind of information.

The two had actually become quite close and had planned to leave Eldsboro to start a new life together. As fate would have it, Ricky wound up behind bars, but Mary promised to wait for him. Ricky's depression deepened every time she left and with each disappointing report from his lawyer.

Mary's visits were essential to Ricky's mental well-being and for his physical health, because he often refused to eat for days. She encouraged him and helped him to look down the road to much happier times, when they would be together. She had an unusually strong conviction that his lawyer would one day find that vital piece of the puzzle that would get Ricky a new trial and eventually freedom from prison. Ricky often asked how she could be so sure that proof would surface.

She would always respond, "My love, don't you know that you didn't kill Mr. Lowry?"

After Ricky answered, "Yes," she would always reply, "Well, that's why I am so sure."

Mary had confidence about his innocence, because on the night of the murder of Mr. Lowry, she had been working the late shift at the diner. On her walk home, she saw someone other than Ricky leaving the shop area. She recognized him but she did not know about the Mr. Lowry's death until the next day when she also found out that Ricky had been detained in connection with the fire. Mr. Lowry's death had not yet been ruled a homicide.

She followed the man for a couple of blocks since it paralleled her route back to her apartment. When she got to within a half a block of the man, he crossed behind a street lamp. It was Mr. Felton. He proceeded on, and Mary turned to her right at the front entrance of her complex. She went in and did not think much about seeing him until Lieutenant Lingren questioned her days later at the diner.

She kept quiet about seeing Felton that night, and the lieutenant didn't ask her about anything other than the argument she overheard in the diner between Ricky and Johnny. That was the second time he had questioned her about the argument, but she gave no additional information about that either. She decided not to tell Ricky for an even more sinister reason. It turns out that long before she met Ricky and long before Lily became involved with Felton, she had a secret affair with Dan Felton.

They kept it a secret for two years, mainly because Dan didn't think Mary fit into the niche of friends that he perceived he had.

Mary was relatively poor and accepted the advances of Mr. Felton with reservation, because she considered herself to be a good, moral person. She reasoned that as long as it was a mutually advantageous relationship, then what was the harm?

Mr. Felton lavished expensive gifts on her like jewelry and clothing. Mary was an attractive lady and could have certainly had any number of eligible men in Eldsboro, but sometimes things just happen. Their time together was usually shared on trips out of town, where their circles of friends could not see them.

Eventually, Mary tired of Felton's controlling behavior, even though he continued to give her the gifts including lots of money. She saved almost all of the money and part of the gifts went into storage, because she couldn't wear them. If she did, everyone would ask where she got them.

Mary was becoming more and more distant from Dan each time they met. Then, one day she announced that she did not want to see him anymore. He was furious, but he had tired of the association, also. Besides, he had spotted a much younger and prettier young girl, who would soon take Mary's place in his warped, middle-aged heart. It was Lily Owens.

He told Mary that if she ever told anyone about their romance he would smear her name all over the city and he promised to see to it that she would never get another job in Eldsboro.

Mary had saved enough money from her job and Felton's gifts over the two years they were together, but she wanted to stay in Eldsboro. She had made some good friends, so she abided by his blackmail and said nothing even after Ricky was charged with the murder of Mr. Lowry. However, her relationship with Ricky would soon cause her to have urges to tell everything she knew about the night of the murder.

Unlike her connection with Dan Felton, she and Ricky became so much more than casual lovers, despite their wide difference in age. Now, Mary would have to make a decision between what was sure to be a campaign of hate from her former provider and the young man who had vowed unending love for her. She could not and would not be silent any longer about seeing Felton on that night that seemed so long ago. It was a surprisingly easy choice for her. It was the only way she and Ricky would ever be together.

She visited Ricky the next day after making her life-changing decision. After greeting each other through the glass petition, Mary placed her hands on the glass.

As he mirrored her hands with his, Mary looked into his eyes, then dropped her head and said, "Ricky, I have something to tell you, and I want you to promise that you will hear me out. okay?"

"Of course. What is it?" Ricky asked.

"I think I know something that will clear you of the murder of Mr. Lowry."

"That's wonderful, Mary." Ricky interrupted.

"Wait a minute." Mary said. "Wait a minute, my love … let me finish."

Ricky put his hand over his mouth and motioned for her to go ahead, as he mimed zipping his mouth shut and giving a hand signal showing that he swore to be quiet.

"You see, before I met you, Dan … I mean, Mr. Felton and I went together for a long time. He helped me out a lot, but he made me swear to never tell anyone about our relationship after we went our separate ways."

"He had some sort of hold on you, too!" exclaimed Ricky.

"I'm afraid he did, but there is something more." she said. "I saw him almost running from the Shop area the night of the murder."

"Do you mean that you have let me sit here in this horrible place all this time with evidence like that?" Ricky questioned.

"Please believe me Ricky," she replied. "I was scared, because I thought he might hurt me … especially if he was the one who killed Mr. Lowry. But, you and I have something special, and I don't care what happens to me, if this thing keeps us apart."

She started crying.

Ricky broke down too and apologized to her for not seeing her plight.

They talked a little more about the situation and what Ricky wanted Mary to do before the guard told them that their visitation time was done.

Mary met with Ben Applegate the next day and told him the about her relationship with Dan Felton and what she had seen that night.

Ben agreed that this was probably the evidence that he had been looking for all along. He said that it might be enough to get the retrial and possibly get Ricky out of prison for good. His time for the arson conviction was almost up, so the timing was perfect.

He filed a third time for the new trial, and Judge Branton granted the appeal. The trial date was set for two weeks after Christmas which coincided exactly with the end of Ricky's sentence for the fire.

Ben contacted the District Attorney's office, and they immediately told the Police Department to reopen the case.

When Lieutenant Lingren heard about the new evidence, he called Mary Crenshaw in for questioning.

He compared the time she had seen Mr. Felton leaving the scene of the murder with the coroner's report of the time of death, and it coincided within the timeframe that would place him there and made him a primary suspect.

Dan Felton came in next to be interrogated by the lieutenant. *I'll have that would-be Sherlock Holmes' badge before this is through,* he thought as he pushed open the door to Lieutenant Lingren's office.

"You had better have a really good reason for bringing me down here again, Mister." growled Mr. Felton. "What is so all-fired important that you had to bother me again now?"

"I think that *murder* is pretty important, don't you?" the lieutenant asked sarcastically. "The murder of Mr. Lowry."

"Now, wait just a darn minute … that whole matter was settled with the trial a long time ago." replied Mr. Felton. "You had better get down to what this has to do with me, or I will see to it that you are removed from this case!"

"If you will settle down and be quiet for a second, I will tell you exactly what it has to do with you. May I continue?" asked Lieutenant Lingren.

"Go ahead then … I'm waiting." blurted Felton impatiently.

"Okay, we have a new witness in the case. This witness saw someone leaving the scene of the crime within a few minutes after the murder took place."

"So?" replied Felton.

"So ... the person they saw was you!" the lieutenant said in his best accusatory tone.

"Me? That's the most ridiculous thing I have ever heard." replied Felton. "Did that no good nephew of mine come up with this blatant lie to get out of jail?"

"No, no ... Ricky has never said one word against you the whole time he's been in prison." answered the lieutenant. "It was Mary Crenshaw who saw you that night. You didn't see her, but she saw you. Now, what do you have to say about that?"

Mr. Felton almost fell out of his chair when he heard that his former lover was the witness against him.

He stammered and finally said, "I will not say one more word on the matter. I will have my lawyer tell you what I have to say about that ... understand?"

"As you will. I will let you know when we will need you again. And, by the way, don't leave town. I have a feeling that there will be lots more questions for you and your lawyer in the near future."

Mr. Felton stormed out of the interrogation room, and then the waiting room, and then the precinct slamming each door harder as he went. The lieutenant sat for a few minutes in his chair pondering what had just occurred. A feeling of strange satisfaction came over him and a wry smile was followed by a short, quick chuckle. He knew that those doubts he had all along about Ricky's involvement in the murder might soon be resolved. He went back to his office and finished the report on the interrogation of Mr. Felton.

Chapter 13

A Winter of Holidays

The autumn painted the landscape with refreshing, bright colors, and the chilly mornings evolved into cool days with the winds of change in the air.

Elliot did find it difficult, as Lily's father had suggested on Thanksgiving Day, to keep from proposing to Lily until the spring. Christmas was getting close, so the season's chores and festivities helped him put it out of his mind for days at a time, but it was always there for him to ponder in his quiet times. He did wait, however, confirming another one of his assets, patience.

Lily was busy with the season's doings. She thought it would be great if Elliot could get his mother to come to Eldsboro for Christmas Eve and Christmas Day. Her parents were again providing dinner on Christmas Eve and a gigantic feast for Christmas Day. She asked Elliot several times before he finally agreed to ask his mom to come.

A couple of weeks before Christmas, Ms. Timberlake said that she would come, but for Christmas Eve only. She explained that she already had plans for Christmas Day, and that she would have to get up early that morning in order to make her appointment in Columbus on the twenty-fifth.

Elliot did not get an answer from his mother about where she was spending Christmas Day. He figured that if she wanted him to know, she would eventually tell him.

Lily was excited she agreed to come, especially since they had only met once, when she and Elliot visited her months earlier.

It was, in her heart, a big deal. She suspected that Elliot would ask her the "big question" one day, so it was important to get to know the person who brought her future husband into the world. She and her mother planned out the menu with what Elliot told them were Ms. Timberlake's favorite Christmas foods. Luckily, they were the traditional ones that Lily's family had always enjoyed.

Christmas Eve had always been their time for exchanging gifts, so there was no need for any special out-of-the ordinary entertainment. The house was simply dazzling with colored lights, poinsettias, holly, mistletoe, garlands, and a magnificent ten-foot tall, all-natural tree that Elliot and Lily's father had hand-picked from the Christmas tree farm just outside of town. A star of Bethlehem that Lily had made adorned the topmost bough, and lights of every color reflected in the tinsel and glitter that were painstakingly added by Lilly and her mom.

The week before Christmas, before all the festivities began in earnest, Lily and Eliot decided to go on a leisurely drive into the hill country just to get away for a few hours and relax.

They drove the back roads toward Lancaster, and although the autumn colors had long disappeared and a thin coating of pearly white snow blanketed the landscape, the hardwood forests that spread out for miles on both sides of the two-lane roads were stunning and beautiful.

It was a spur-of-the-moment excursion, and neither had paid any attention to the weather forecast before they left home that morning. They would certainly have canceled the outing if they had seen what was in store for them. The area was in for a substantial, but fast-moving snow storm.

As they reached their turn-around point about thirty-five miles from Eldsboro, they noticed that the clouds had thickened and seemed to reach all the way down to the surface of the roadway. Then, it began. First, like frozen mist, then bigger and bigger flakes splattered on the truck's windshield. They came so hard and fast that Elliot's wipers could not keep his view clear to drive.

They pulled over at the first opportunity, where the road widened at an overview point.

Lily voiced her concern. "Elliot, what are we going to do?"

"Don't worry, sweetheart. It is probably just a snow squall … it happens all the time up here. Probably won't last long, and we can be on our way."

Well, after an hour and two inches or more of fresh snow, it was not over. In fact, it seemed to be snowing even harder.

Elliot kept comforting Lily. He had snow tires on his truck and told her that he was pretty good at handling the conditions. He said that he would get going again as soon as the visibility got better. A little later, it did, and they decided to continue on at a very slow, deliberate pace.

By the time they got near the end of the two-lane secondary road they were on, it was apparent that it was not going to be a sure thing that they would get back home before dark.

Lily grabbed her cell phone and called her mom to tell her what was going on and that they were going to try to get back to the Steak Pit restaurant to shelter there. It was only about ten miles away, but that was a long way in such conditions.

When they were about five miles from the main road, the snow had piled up so high that they knew they could not make it all the way to the restaurant. When the truck could not go any farther, they had to decide whether to stick it out in the truck or try to walk the distance to the restaurant, which was now about six miles away.

They ruled out the latter idea and huddled in the truck.

It might not be open anyway. Suddenly, Elliot remembered that the old cabin they had stayed in during the rainstorm the summer before, was only about a mile further down the road.

They decided to give it a chance. They trudged through the snow that was now approaching ten inches deep and finally reached the cabin.

They got in and started a fire in the old pot-bellied stove. Then settled down for what would be a long, cold, snowy but romantic night together.

Lily called her parents to let them know where they were and told them not to worry.

She, of course, got a sermon about proper behavior from her dad. He said that he would get up early in the morning and drive up to meet them. It had only snowed an inch or two in Eldsboro, so it would be no problem for him.

Elliot noticed that the snowflakes began to diminish in size but had become more tightly bunched. His experience had taught him this meant that the storm would be there for quite a while. He was right, and the snow intensified into a full-fledged blizzard. It was coming down at an incredible three inches per hour, and the wind was blowing it sideways forming white-out conditions. It was fortunate that they found the cabin when they did.

There were no outside lights at the cabin or had burned out long ago, so Lily was not aware of the situation completely. Elliot didn't want to alarm her, but he knew he had to tell her. When he got back inside with the wood under his arm, he put a few pieces into the old stove and asked Lily to brace herself.

"Lily, the storm is a lot worse than we thought it was going to be. It is six inches deeper than when we got here and is coming down harder than I have ever seen. You had better call your dad and let him know that we probably won't be able to get back home tomorrow, after all. Let him know that we are alright here. If it keeps piling up like this all night, we could be stuck here for days. Go ahead and call him, and I will look around to see what there is here to eat and drink."

Lily made the call, and her father told her to stay warm until morning. He said that he would get in touch with the wildlife department and ask then to organize a rescue party first thing in the morning.

Mr. Owens did just that and assured Lily that they would do everything they could do to reach them the following day.

The officer told Mr. Owens that the timing of getting to them was dependent on what the storm would allow them to do. They told him that since it was only a few miles off the main highway that it should not be a problem, unless the storm got even worse.

Elliot found some canned goods in the cupboard that hunters, who used the cabin regularly, left behind. There were plenty of pots, pans, and utensils to make things easier to prepare. They also had running water from a deep well on the property.

Lily was obviously worried about the storm and the situation, but she trusted Elliot and his survival skills almost as much as she had grown to love him.

So, they managed to stay warm until morning by cuddling together on the old sofa with a couple of old heavy wool blankets from the bedroom. Elliot was not what you would call a zealous Christian, but his moral values coupled with Lily's vow of celibacy until her wedding night, kept things on the up-and-up through the long night.

However, the two learned a lot about each other and drew even closer than ever. Passionate embraces and kisses warmed them both and solidified their bond until morning came.

As the welcome sun came piercing through the trees around the cabin, the snow glistened and sparkled like diamonds. White tail deer left tell-tale evidence around the backyard, and one giant buck stood on a distant ridge looking back where he had been.

Elliot had been up for a half hour or so and had fixed some coffee. He peered out the back window and spotted the deer standing like a statue of ice. Lily shuffled to her feet, wrapped one of the blankets around her tightly and eased over to the window next to Elliot. He just pointed and they stood there is awe of nature at its best.

The trance was broken as Elliot looked up and sifted through the cans to see what might make a decent breakfast.

"What about that one?" Lily pointed at a can on top of the others.

"Let's see. Yeah, that looks like the ticket ... it's old-fashioned breakfast sausage in a can. My mom used to fix that with grits and hash browns. I haven't had any in a long, long time. And, here are some grits in this glass jar ... might still be good."

"Just one way to find out, I guess." Lily said. "Let's cook it up and see. There is some salt right here, too."

"No potatoes, but that's okay." replied Elliot. "I'll get some water and a pot. You pour in the grits, and I'll stoke the fire."

They got the grits going on the stove and found a can opener to get into the can of sausage. It smelled fine, so they read the label to see how to prepare it. The option they chose was to put it in a frying pan with the juice from the can. The smell of it cooking filled the room and was quite pleasant, indeed.

Lily kept the grits stirred and soon they were ready to try both dishes. She asked if he ate the sausage separately from the grits or mixed it in.

He said that he always mixed the sausage in with the grits.

With a little pinch of salt in the grits, a cup of coffee with a little sugar, they had a breakfast fit for a king and queen. After they finished the feast, they sat on the sofa wrapped in the blankets, sipped their coffee and talked about their future. It was a good time, but then reality came back, when they remembered they were stranded miles from civilization with a foot and a half of snow. The back road that had not seen a snow plow in twenty years and had such steep shoulders that made traveling in Elliot's truck so treacherous, even if it could navigate through the deep snow.

They kept a steady vigil for the wildlife department rescue team.

It was almost noon when three snowmobiles slid up to the front door of the cabin. Wildlife officers were driving all three vehicles, and there was only one passenger. It was Mr. Owens.

He jumped off the back and ran up the steps to grab Lily in a hug only a worried father could give his precious daughter.

Elliot said, "Thanks to all of you. We are sorry to put you to all of this trouble, but the storm caught us off guard. My truck is up the road just around the corner about a half mile back or so."

"We'll worry about the truck later." said Mr. Owens. "The main thing right now is getting you two back to Eldsboro."

The wildlife officers helped them clean up the cabin and put out the fire, and they hopped onto the snow mobiles and headed back to the main road, which had been partially cleared. Their trucks were waiting at the intersection. They loaded the happy youngsters and drove back to town.

They stopped first at Lily's house.

Lily's mom fed them lunch and warmed them up, as she listened to the details of their adventure.

Mr. Owens took Elliot back to his home and offered to take him back to get his truck the next day.

The festivities of Christmas Eve and Christmas Day were still to come and Lily and Elliot's adventure in the snowstorm had taken their attention away from what was about to take place.

Lily and Elliot were anchored a little firmer because of their ordeal. Elliot commented to Lily, "I guess there is something to be said about the security and safety of home, sweet home after going through something like that, Lily."

Lily acknowledged with a quick and affirmative shake of her head.

The incident would stick with them for a long time.

Elliot's mom was quite a hit with Lily and her parents. She shared her story about Elliot's dad, the car accident, and their otherwise perfect life together with her son until that fateful day.

They exchanged gifts and had some homemade eggnog and fruit cake, before Mrs. Timberlake excused herself. She wanted to rest up before her trip to Williston the next day.

Lily and Elliot said goodbye to her on Christmas morning. They stood and waved until she got out of sight. They returned inside and had a great Christmas feast a little later. It was a wonderful day. They had the assurance that Mrs. Timberlake was on-board with Elliot's engagement to Lily, and the fact that Lily's parents had taken well to their daughter's future mother-in-law. The day ended about as well as could have been expected.

Chapter 14

Secret Plans

Ricky spent the holidays staring cell walls and the cell across from his. Mary came by to see him on Christmas Eve and stayed with him for an extra half hour beyond normal visiting hours. The extra time was allowed because of the holidays. They talked a lot about what they might do if and when Ricky was acquitted of the murder of Mr. Lowry. The retrial was set for mid-January, so their plans had a little more urgency and became more specific.

"Let's just get out of this place, Ricky." Mary said. "After all this, it won't be the same, and when they find out about you and me, people won't treat us the same anymore."

"I have been thinking the same thing. What do you think about moving to Florida?" Ricky asked. "I have heard that the panhandle area around Destin and Panama City are really great. And, there is plenty of work, etc."

"That sounds pretty good to me." Mary said. "Wish we could leave tomorrow."

"Me too! But, we still have quite a way to go here before we can get to there. And, you know, I have been thinking about something else. You said that you saw my uncle leaving the shop area that night. Are you sure he did not see you?"

"Yes, I am sure." she replied.

"Well, just to be safe, I want you to stay away from him until the trial," Ricky insisted, "Promise me that, Mary."

"I promise, but I think that maybe I will take Lieutenant Lingren up on his suggestion that I be placed in protective custody." Mary said.

"Great! That is just what you should do." Ricky said with a sigh. "We only have a few weeks until the trial."

Mary went to see the lieutenant the next day, and she was placed in a holding cell. It was the general practice of the department to house people in protective custody in a well-guarded, fenced-in apartment complex they maintained for such occasions, but they were being renovated, and they asked her to use the cell away from the main area where the inmates were housed. She had all she needed to get by until the time came to testify. Luckily, she had two weeks of vacation time, so she used that at the restaurant to relieve any suspicions from her boss.

Dan Felton had begun his preparations, too. His lawyer, Christopher Rollins, had amassed piles of paper work that would supposedly clear his client of any wrongdoing. Within that bunch of files was one marked "Mary Crenshaw's past". It contained every bit of dirt that he could scrape up against Mary. Most of it was hearsay evidence about affairs and claims made by fellow workers from her days in Cincinnati, where she had also been a waitress for many years.

Felton was forbidden from seeing or speaking to Mary, but he had family connections within the police department.

Despite his lawyer's instructions to stay home and to avoid confrontations with anyone, especially those associated with the case, Felton went around town making threats and telling everyone that he would not be convicted of any crime.

Lieutenant Lingren received a call from the owner of the diner where Mary worked. The owner, Mr. Pinnozzi complained that Felton had been in his place asking questions about Mary and just plain harassing his customers.

The lieutenant paid Felton a visit early one afternoon at his home and found him to be his usual, belligerent self.

The lieutenant told him that if he did not stop bothering people that he would have him arrested for doing so.

Of course, Felton countered by telling Lieutenant Lingren that he would have his lawyer contact the department and have him suspended.

The lieutenant told him to go ahead and that he would see him in court.

"You just heed what I have told you about harassing those people at the restaurant and Mary, too," ordered the lieutenant as he excused himself and left.

Felton sat on the hearth of his fireplace. He was smoldering more than the dying embers in the logs. He pondered his next move. He thought that if he could get to Mary and find out what she knew, he might be able get her to remain quiet, leave town, or change what she was going to say in court. He had to think of a way to stop her from incriminating him.

So, he set about doing just that. He petitioned his lawyer, Christopher Rollins, to find out what Mary was going to testify to in court.

Mr. Rollins already had the written statement in his files, but he had not shown it to Felton.

He already knew how vindictive and impulsive Felton could be.

It was late the next day when Rollins came over and showed Felton the statement. It said that Mary had seen Felton running from the scene of the crime that night … now such a long time ago. He told Felton that he would try to set up a meeting between his client and Mary the next day, so that he could try to persuade her.

Sure enough, Mr. Rollins did arrange the meeting. Felton came in the back way, so that no one could see him with the exception of a very specific officer, who let him in and out of the cell.

Mary seemed shocked and visibly afraid when the officer unlocked her cell door and let Felton come inside with her.

"Officer, officer. What is going on here … I don't want this man in here." pleaded Mary, "Please get him out of here this minute!"

"Calm down, Miss Crenshaw. I'll be right over there if you need me for anything." replied the officer.

"I'm not going to hurt you, Mary." Mr. Felton said. "I just want to find out why you have said that you saw me the night of the murder … to see if we can straighten this thing out."

"I don't have anything to say to you. I told you to stay away from me and I meant it!" shouted Mary. "Now, go … just go!"

"I'll go, but first give me two minutes. Then I will go and not bother you ever again." Felton insisted.

The "ever again" part of what Felton said convinced Mary to let him have his say. "Go ahead, then, but then you get out of here … you understand?"

"Okay, okay. I've heard what you said about seeing me that night, but I was with someone until well after midnight, and then I went straight home."

"I did see you, Dan. I even followed you to make sure it was you." Mary replied. It was you alright. I saw you go down an alley. That's when I turned around and went home. It was you alright! Then I found out about the murder the next day and figured out that you had killed Mr. Lowry."

"Mary, if you tell that in court, they will convict me of murder; don't you see?" Mr. Felton asked.

"Yes, I know they will, because you did it!" she yelled loudly.

"But Mary, you and I … I mean we had something once. How could you turn on me this way?" He asked.

"Turn on you? How about how you turned on Ricky? You were going to let him rot in prison for something you did." Mary said as she started to cry.

"I never meant for Ricky to get in trouble, but he should have taken care of Lowry himself." Felton stopped in mid-sentence, when he realized that he had all but confessed to Mary that he was the killer. He remembered the officer was standing only a few feet away and probably heard every word he said.

"See, I knew you did it." said Mary.

"Mary, can't we come to some kind of agreement about this?" pleaded Mr. Felton. "I know. I have some money put back for my retirement. I will give you as much of it as you want, if you will just say it was not me you saw that night. What do you say, Mary … for old time's sake?"

Mary couldn't believe she even considered it for a minute, but she told Felton, "No, and you can be assured that I will tell my lawyer and this, too."

Felton realized that Mary was not going to budge and called for the bailiff to let him out of the cell. He handed him a hundred-dollar bill on the way out and went back to his house to think about his next move. The officer had been assigned to this duty by Felton's cousin, who worked in the department.

Chapter 15

Ricky's Retrial

The day of the retrial arrived, and the county courthouse was packed to capacity. Ricky's parents were there, of course, along with Lily and Elliot, Mr. Felton, Johnny Owens and his parents, and even the Reverend Johnson. Mary Crenshaw was there, too. She sat way back in a corner accompanied by a deputy.

Judge Branton, who presided at the first trial, had recused himself for personal reasons from the retrial. Judge Parker Garrison came in and took his seat.

The officer of the court called everyone to order and told all to be seated.

Judge Garrison was a veteran of thirty years on the bench. He was considered to be fair but tough. Both lawyers thought that they had a slight advantage by having him on the bench for the trial.

Ricky's lawyer, Ben Applegate, felt that his client would get the benefit of the doubt in rulings made by the judge because of his reputation of fairness.

On the other hand, the prosecution thought that the advantage was in their favor. Ricky had already been convicted of the murder of Robert Lowry and for arson in burning the shop building. That evidence, whether circumstantial or concrete, was already part of the court record, and they could refer to that information as they needed.

In his opening remarks, Ben Applegate reminded the jury that most of that evidence was circumstantial. This case now revolved around what he called, "a startling new piece of evidence that would clear Ricky of the murder of Mr. Lowry without a doubt in the world."

He told them, "When you hear this new witness, you must find my client, Ricky Pendleton, innocent of the crime of murder. He has been in prison for more than a year for a crime he did not commit." He thanked the court and yielded to the prosecutor for his opening remarks.

The prosecutor for the county, Bill Weber, slid around his table, shaking his head and snickering.

"My eloquent counterpart, Mr. Applegate, has delivered quite a speech to you about new evidence in this case, but let me remind you of the preponderance of evidence that convicted his client in the first trial. The prosecution will, with all assurance, refute whatever testimony the defense conjures up, and we will show you that their witness should not be believed because of several reasons that will become quite apparent as we proceed. I ask that you listen to all of the evidence and that you rule to keep this young man behind bars, where he belongs. Thank you."

The prosecution's case opened with Bill Weber calling Lieutenant Charles Lingren to the stand.

He began by asking him, "Did you question Ricky Pendleton about the fire at any time during your investigation?"

"Yes." replied Lieutenant Lingren.

"And, did Ricky admit that he started the shop fire?" Mr. Weber asked.

"Yes, he did admit to starting the fire. He said he was very upset about getting a bad grade from Mr. Lowry on a school project and wanted to do something that would get back at him for that, but he also said that he did not kill Mr. Lowry …"

Mr. Weber interrupted. "Please just stick to answering my questions about the fire. Your Honor, I ask that the lieutenant's last statement be stricken from the record!"

Judge Garrison rested his chin on his hand for a moment and said, "I am sure we will get to that part of the questioning later. The witness will provide answers to the questions asked, and the jury will disregard the last part of his answer."

On cross-examination, Ben Applegate picked up on that point by asking the lieutenant to continue his statement regarding Ricky's confession.

"Yes, as I was saying," replied the lieutenant, "Ricky actually came in voluntarily to the police station and admitted to the arson. After that, he told me that he did not know what had happened after Mr. Lowry confronted him at the shop. He told me that when he left, Mr. Lowry was perfectly okay"

"And did you believe him, lieutenant?"

Before he could answer, the prosecutor stood up quickly and loudly stated, "I object, Your Honor. The counselor is asking for a conclusion on the part of the witness ... it will be up to the jury to decide whether to believe the defendant or not."

The judge held up one hand and motioned for Mr. Weber to calm down. "Mr. Applegate, the prosecutor has a point well taken. Please refrain from that line of questioning. Now proceed."

The lieutenant was excused and the prosecutor was asked to call his next witness.

After three more witnesses and testimony from forensic experts from the first trial, he stated that he had no more witnesses and the prosecution rested.

Ben Applegate stood and opened his defense by calling Mary Crenshaw to the stand. As she walked from the back of the court room, she made eye contact with Lily and Elliot who were there with Johnny.

She looked to her right, as she approached the lawyer's desks, and she saw Mr. Felton with his head down refusing to look at her.

She thought to herself as she rounded the railing and stood for the swearing in, *I can't let Dan get away with it. I must tell the truth no matter how much it hurts.*

She took her seat. Ben Applegate stood directly in front of her with both hands on the railing in front of Mary. "Ms. Crenshaw, can you please tell the court what you do for a living and where you work?"

"I am a waitress down at the coffee shop on Bramble Street," replied Mary. "I have been there for about six years now."

"And were you working on the night of May 3, two years ago?" asked Mr. Applegate.

"Yes, I was." Mary stated.

"And can you tell us what you saw on that particular evening?" Mr. Applegate scanned the jury and around the courtroom finishing with Dan Felton then the Judge.

"I got off work just after midnight. We closed at eleven thirty, but since it was Friday night, I had some extra clean-up to do. I always close up for Mr. Pinozzi on Fridays, so he can get home. He takes care of his mother, who is very ill. Anyway, I locked the front door and left by the back door. As I turned to walk toward the street where I live-Laurel Street, I saw someone coming out of the burned-out area near the high school shop. It seemed a little peculiar to me, so I watched as that person hurried down the far side of the street, going in the same direction I was going."

"And, could you make out who that person was, Ms. Crenshaw?" Mr. Applegate asked.

"I most certainly could … it was Dan Felton."

Mr. Weber objected immediately. "Your Honor, Mr. Felton is not on trial here!"

The judge looked to Mr. Applegate and instructed him to get to the point with the witness, or he would sustain the prosecution's objection.

"Yes, Your Honor." Mr. Applegate said. "It will become quite obvious why all of this is relevant and a vital part of our case for the defense. Now, Ms. Crenshaw, are you sure it was Mr. Dan Felton you saw that night?"

"Yes, absolutely: It was Dan." she said emphatically.

Ben turned to face the jury. "This is an eyewitness who is telling us that she saw someone other than Ricky Pendleton leaving the scene of the murder of Mr. Lowry on the night of the murder. We have now established reasonable doubt and placed someone other than Ricky at the scene."

There were oohs and ahs from all over the courtroom.

Mr. Felton kept his head down and slouched a little deeper into his chair.

Mr. Applegate said, "Your Honor, I would like to yield to the prosecutor, but would like to reserve the right to recall Ms. Crenshaw at a later time."

The judge confirmed his approval of that motion and called on the prosecution to cross-examine the witness.

Mr. Weber almost jumped out of his chair at his chance to question Mary.

"Ms. Crenshaw," he began. "Can you tell me how you know Dan Felton?"

"Well ..." she hesitated and took a deep breath. "We dated for a while a few years ago."

"For a while?" He asked. "Isn't it true that you and Mr. Felton dated for almost two years?"

"That's correct ... for about two years." Mary replied.

"And are you still friends, Ms. Crenshaw?"

"No, I would not say that we are friends."

"Oh, I see. Well, isn't it a fact, Ms. Crenshaw, that you hate Mr. Felton? Didn't you tell him to never call you again and that you never wanted to see him again? And didn't you take thousands of dollars' worth of gifts from him during those two years?"

"Yes, yes I guess I did." Mary said sheepishly.

Mr. Weber glanced toward the jury. "And, aren't you now involved with none other than Ricky Pendleton, the defendant?"

"I love Ricky very much?" Mary said "But that has nothing to do with what I saw that night." She began to cry.

"Well, maybe you are just making up this story to protect your new lover?" implied Mr. Weber.

"Now just a minute!" Ben Applegate shouted. "Your Honor, not only is the prosecution badgering this witness, but he is jumping to his own conclusions!"

The judge sustained Ben's objection and directed Mr. Weber to stop harassing Ms. Crenshaw.

Mr. Weber became quite agitated. He paced back and forth in front of the jury, then turned toward Mary. He walked quickly towards her with his hands clasped behind him.

"Ms. Crenshaw, I was hoping not to have to do this, but since you insist on saying you saw Dan Felton that night, I must ask you some questions that will probably make you very uncomfortable."

"First of all," he continued. "Before you came to Eldsboro, what was your line of work in Cincinnati?"

"Well, I was a waitress for a while." Mary answered.

"A waitress? Is that all? What other jobs did you have there? Please tell us everything!" insisted Mr. Weber.

Ben stood up and objected to the line of questioning that the prosecutor was pursuing,

"Your Honor, I don't see what all of this has to do with the murder of Robert Lowry."

The judge said, "What is the relevance of this? I would like to know myself?"

"Judge Garrison, my line of questioning will establish the lack of credibility of this witness. If you will permit me to continue?" asked the prosecutor.

The judge overruled the defense attorney's objection and instructed Mr. Weber to continue.

"Now, Ms. Crenshaw, will you please answer my question fully? What other jobs or professions did you have in Cincinnati besides being a waitress?"

Mary knew that a full disclosure would probably discredit her testimony thus far, but despite lots of mistakes in her life, she was an honest person who detested liars. "I was a hostess at a nightclub called the Fringe on Top on the east side of town."

"By *hostess*, don't you mean you were a call girl, Ms. Crenshaw?" Weber asked. "And remember that you are still under oath."

Mary hesitated but answered, "Yes … yes, I was." She dropped her head and was excused from the witness stand.

Ben Applegate knew this was going to come up in Mary's testimony. He wanted to ask her a few more questions about that period in her life, but he decided that he should wait, since Mary was so obviously upset by what she had revealed.

Dan Felton got up from his seat suddenly right after Mary got back to her seat and walked out of the courtroom in a bit of a tizzy.

He did not miss much of the trial, because after directing the jury not to discuss the case with anyone overnight, the judge adjourned court for the day.

Lily, Johnny, and Elliot lingered after court was let out, talking and about what strange turn could happen next in the trial.

Johnny mentioned that he was more hopeful than ever that Ricky would be acquitted of the murder of Mr. Lowry.

Elliot patted him on the back and said, "Johnny, I think things are going to be okay now … you'll see."

Lily got between the two and grabbed Johnny's hand on one side and Elliot's on the other. They left the court room followed by Mr. and Mrs. Owens. Mr. and Mrs. Pendleton were right behind them.

As they neared the courtroom doors, they all glanced over ay Mary, who was still sitting next to the officer. She was crying and shaking her head. They heard her say between her tears, "I thought all of that life was behind me. I hoped that Eldsboro would be the start of a new life for me."

Chapter 16

Change in a Black Heart

Dan Felton did not go straight home when he left the court house. He went down to his office at the sawmill. He sat in his chair behind his desk for a half hour or more, then pulled out a writing pad from the center drawer of his desk.

Mary's testimony was the final straw in causing Dan to finally admit to himself that he had done some awful things in his life. Mary was someone who actually did mean something to him, and now she was telling the whole world what he now realized about himself. He thought about what might lie ahead for him. He could not see spending the rest of his life in prison. His career at the lumber company was over for sure, even if he were to be acquitted of Mary's accusations.

He reasoned that there was only one thing left to do. He picked up a red felt-tip pen from the mason jar on the right-hand corner of his computer table and began to write a note.

He addressed it to Lieutenant Lingren.

It read: "This is to let you know that Mary was right. She did see me leaving the shop site that night. I went there to make sure that Ricky destroyed anything that could connect him to the fire.

When I got there, I stayed out of sight. Ricky and Robert Lowry were talking in the middle of all the rubble. I couldn't hear what they were saying, but I guessed that Lowry knew that Ricky had set the fire. I really thought that Ricky would take care of him right then and there, but HE DID NOT! He just walked away.

So, I decided that I would have to do something myself. I eased over to Robert and hit him as hard as I could with a piece of steel rebar I found on the ground. I had to make sure he was dead, so I hit him again and then again. I threw that piece of metal into the dumpster several blocks away.

Besides, Robert knew that I had done some things in my past that I couldn't let come to light. He and I were good friends a long time ago. This way, I thought I was helping Ricky and myself, too.

I am truly sorry I did this awful thing to him and his family. I am also sorry that I told the prosecutor about Mary's past. I made up some of it. She really changed her life around when she came to Eldsboro. She is a wonderful lady. I really do love her.

When you get this note, I will be gone. Please let Ricky, Mary, and even young Elliot know that I am sorry too."

He signed it Daniel Felton.

He placed it in a company envelope, sealed it, addressed it to the lieutenant, and hand carried it to the police station. He asked the officer at the desk to make sure that Lieutenant Lingren got it the next morning.

Dan then returned to the sawmill. He climbed to the highest point of the conveyor system and then up the catwalks and stairs to the highest chip cyclone. He stood there looking out over the mill site. He reminisced about his life for a few minutes.

He remembered the missed opportunities in his life to do the right thing. He certainly had done wrong by the many women in his life Lily Owens, Mary Crenshaw, and others.

Maybe, if I had been a little gentler. I guess that I was just too selfish with them and maybe with a lot of things in my life. And besides, there is nothing left for me here now. This will be best for everyone concerned.

Oh well, maybe this will make up for some of the bad things I have done. I have made a mess out of everything. Even down at the sawmill, it will only be a matter of time, before my superiors find out that I had been forging the records concerning my bonuses.

Just then, he saw one of the night-shift security guards coming up the catwalks below him. He moved over closer to the catwalk railing. He shook his head, let out a scream and then, with a final deep breath, jumped over the railing, falling four stories to his death.

The security guard had spotted him before he jumped, but it was too late to stop him. There was no way that anyone could survive a fall from that height, and he did not. The guard immediately called 911 from his cell phone. The EMT vehicles arrived at about the same time as the police did.

Lieutenant Lingren had been called in and was at the mill a few minutes later.

Mr. Felton was pronounced dead immediately by the medics and the medical examiner.

The lieutenant questioned the security guard and after the scene was secured, he decided to go back to his office to do his report while the details were still fresh in his mind.

When he arrived, he was handed Dan's note. He went into his office, sat down, and opened the envelope.

His mouth fell open as he read what amounted to a full confession of the murder of Robert Lowry by Dan Felton, and in fact, served as a suicide note.

Lieutenant Lingren realized that this also proved that Ricky Pendleton was innocent of that same crime. He completed his report on Felton's death and alerted Ricky's attorney as well as the prosecutor about Felton's note.

In court the next afternoon, Ben Applegate asked the judge to let him present the new evidence.

The judge informed the jury about Mr. Felton's death and directed the defense to go ahead with the new information.

Ben turned to the judge and jury and said, "I am holding a note written by Daniel Felton, addressed to Lieutenant Lingren. It was written before Mr. Felton's death last night at the sawmill."

He read it slowly and distinctly, so that the jury could understand each word. He then turned to the judge and asked that the charges against his client, Ricky Pendleton, be dropped immediately.

The judge paused for a few seconds and then asked the prosecutor if he had any objections to Ben's request.

Mr. Weber said, "No, Your Honor ... no objections."

There were sighs from all over the courtroom, as the judge dismissed the jury. He looked directly at Ricky and said, "Mr. Pendleton, you are free to go, and the court humbly apologizes for the obvious inconvenience and hardship you have gone through because of this mistake. Good luck to you, young man. This court is adjourned."

Ricky and his parents met behind the defense's table in a group hug.

Ben Applegate patted Ricky on the back, as he grabbed his briefcase and moved out of the way.

Ricky looked up and saw Mary walking towards him. He broke clear of his parents and sprinted to meet her in the aisle. They embraced, kissed, and walked out together with his parents, Elliot, Johnny, and Lily celebrating as they went.

Chapter 17

In the Garden

A couple of weeks after Ricky's retrial, Elliot refocused on his plan to ask Lily to marry him in the spring in his garden. The winter held on well into April, but the lush new green leaves were preceded by aromatic blossoms on the wild flowering trees and understory plants. Green shoots overtook the dormant beige-colored grasses, and wildflowers dotted the rolling landscape all around.

The garden was showing signs of life as well. He planted all his normal vegetables and some ornamental, ones he thought would add to the ambience of the atmosphere he had dreamed about having when he proposed to Lily.

He laid out large flat stones down the center of one of the spaces between the rows of plants. In a really pretty, shady area of the garden, he placed a large arbor that was adorned with several varieties of roses. He had not used an artist's brush, but when he finished and had it ready for the big day, it was truly a work of art.

When Elliot was finally ready to propose, he invited Lily on an early dinner date on a Friday in the first part of April. They went to their favorite place, The Steak Pit. His excuse to Lily about going to dinner so early was that he just wanted to get back to his house right before sunset. The time had changed back, so dusk would be around seven o'clock.

They had a great meal and drove back home. It was already getting dark, and the first thing Lily noticed were some lights at the rear of the house in an area near the garden. She asked Elliot if they had been there all along, and he told her that he had just installed them a few weeks earlier so that he could do some work at night in the garden.

He assured her that there was nothing wrong.

"Lily, I've got something to show you out back." He took her hand and led her to the edge of the garden where the new stones marked the walkway through the middle of the rows of crops.

"Elliot, you surely have been doing some work out here … it is just beautiful." she said. "But why in the world did you put these stones here?"

"Just walk along them with me, and you will see." Elliot said. "Come on, sweetheart. You see, these are smooth stones, not stumbling blocks.

As they continued along the stones, Lily reached out her free hand and touched some of the plants that were over knee-high, some with flowers that she would later see as symbols of their coming lifelong committment.

Elliot's hand was a little moist from his nervous sweat. He kept pulling it away from Lily to dry it on his pant leg. He took deep breaths until they reached the end of the stones at the arbor.

They stopped there. Lily looked from one end of the arbor over the top and down the other side at the foliage and magnificent roses that were illuminated by the lights that had been perfectly situated to show their beauty.

Elliot turned to face Lily and grabbed her other hand.

He looked straight into her languid eyes and said, "Lily, I know that the past few months have not been easy for you, but you and I have had some good times. The first day I saw you was right here in this very garden. I thought then, as I do now, that there was something very special about you. You are the most beautiful girl I have ever seen."

His voice cracked a little. "I have found out since that day that you are even more beautiful inside."

He held her closer to him. As he did, he slowly kneeled to one knee.

Looking up to her, he said, "Lily, my love, will you make my life complete and make me the happiest man on the face of the earth? Will you be my wife?"

He pulled out a small box, opened it, and offered her the engagement ring he had bought months before.

"Oh, Elliot. I do love you so much, too, and yes, yes, yes, I will marry you!"

She held out her left hand and he slid the ring onto her finger. He stood and pulled her up to him, and they kissed a kiss for the ages.

Chapter 18

A Proper Waltz

Long before Elliot's proposal, Lily had dreamed of her wedding day. She had imagined the whole ceremony and the reception, how it would look and how she would feel. In her mind, the day just had to be like a fairy tale with all the traditional bells, whistles, and frills to make it something she and Elliot would remember all the days of their lives.

Among those things were a beautiful dress and veil, flower girls tossing rose petals behind her and her father as they walked to traditional music down the aisle, a youngster as the ring bearer, her best buddies as her bridesmaids, the familiar vows by the preacher, and a proper formal waltz with her husband at the reception.

Lily had been a little sheltered from the world of modern pop and rock music because of her parents' religious beliefs, but in her late teen years, she did pick up many of the "in" dance moves of her generation. Of course, that did not include any ballroom dancing.

A few days after Elliot's proposal, she began to organize her thoughts about the wedding. Lily talked to her mom about the reception.

"Mom, I was wondering about my dance with Elliot. Did you know that I have always wanted to do a waltz?"

"Of course, you used to tell me about that even before you were in high school. You called it a real waltz. I think you meant that you wanted it to be done the way the ballroom dancers do it," replied Mrs. Owens.

"Yes, Mom. A proper waltz," Lily continued. "I have been practicing in front of the big mirror in my room for years … just in case the day ever came."

"I know!" Mrs. Owens said with a wry smile.

"What do you mean?" asked Lily,

"Lily … after all, I am your mother. I do live in the same house … remember?" I have ears and eyes. Sometimes I came up the stairs to bring your clean clothes up from the laundry, and I would see you dancing to music I didn't even know you had ever heard let alone liked to play."

"You were spying on me!" Lily said in a slightly elevated tone.

"Of course not, sweetie," Mrs. Owens said. "I would see that you were busy and probably did not want to be disturbed, so I would just leave the clothes outside your door, that's all."

"I'm sorry, Mom. You and Dad have always treated me fairly and never pushed your beliefs on me. You let me explore things to a certain extent. But, what do I do about the dance with Elliot?" Asked Lily.

"First, you have a dance with your father. Believe it or not, he is a great slow dancer. All you have to do is let him lead you. It will be just fine!" Now, I would talk to Elliot and let him know how you feel about doing the waltz. Have you two ever danced on any of your dates?"

"Well, yes and no, I guess." Lily said. "We have slow danced, as you call it, after dinner a couple of times. He is coordinated enough alright, but I don't know if he can do a proper waltz."

"And, if he doesn't know how, why not just ask him to take some lessons with you, and you can teach him a few things yourself, I'm sure." said Mrs. Owens.

"I will do that. As a matter of fact, I need the lessons even if he doesn't. I want to do it the right way. I know that it's not the most important part of the day, and if he doesn't think it is necessary or is too shy to do it, I will not try to force him to take the lessons."

They talked more about the other things they needed to do for the wedding and called Mrs. Timberlake long distance to get her advice on some things as well. They also called Lily's girl friends to confirm commitments for being bridesmaids, etc.

That night, Elliot called to see how Lily was doing with the planning. She filled him in on what she, her mom, and his mom had discussed. Elliot reported that he had been in touch with two of his friends, who agreed to be his groomsmen. They worked with Elliot down at the sawmill.

Lily was anxious to bring up the reception and her concerns about the dance.

She was just about to mention it, when Elliot said, "Sweetheart, have you given any thought to our dance ... what kind of music you want to dance to and all that?"

Lily replied after a short pause to catch her breath, "Actually, Elliot, I have thought about that a lot for most of my life. I would love it, if we could to a Viennese waltz."

"Are you kidding me?" Elliot replied instantly. "I love the waltz. I will be honest with you. I don't know the difference between a Viennese waltz and the Waltz of the Sugarplum Fairies, but if that is something you want, my love, then I am more than willing to learn."

"Actually, I need to learn too." replied Lily. "I have practiced my version of a waltz in my room for years, but I want to do a proper waltz with you at our wedding."

"Looks like we just need to take some lessons, doesn't it?" asked Elliot.

"Oh, Elliot, you are the dearest person I have ever met." If it is alright, I will check around and see if there are any classes available that we can take right away."

"Absolutely, go right ahead. Try to make it after six p.m. or on the weekends, so it doesn't interfere with our work hours." Elliot said.

Lily went straight to her computer after Elliot's phone call and found a couple of classes on ballroom dancing. One would begin in a week and the other one would start in two weeks. Both lasted for three months and were not specifically designed for learning waltzes. Next, she checked into a private dance school on the west side of Eldsboro that offered private one-on-one classes. She looked through the on-line information and noticed that one of the teachers specialized in waltzes. She took down the phone number and called right away.

A deep male voice answered, "Hello. This is Chivalry Dance Studios. I am Willem Strausburg. How may I help you?"

"Yes, my name is Lily Owens, and my fiancé and I need to learn a Viennese waltz right away. Do you have any openings for lessons in the near future? We are getting married in May and want to dance it at our reception."

"It just happens, Miss Owens, that I teach that class. In fact, it is my specialty, and I am open to take students this coming week," replied Mr. Strausburg. "The Viennese is a beautiful, fluid, magical dance, when it is done properly. I can teach you if you will promise me that you will try to do it the way I show you."

"That is exactly why I am calling. I want to learn the right way," Lily replied.

"In that case, when can you start? I am available on Monday through Wednesday mornings from seven until eleven and on Thursday and Friday evenings from seven until eleven." Mr. Strausburg continued. "It will take two sessions per week for a month to teach you. My fee is thirty dollars per hour. Do either of you have any ballroom dancing experience?"

"I'm afraid not, but I think we are both quick learners. May we start next Thursday night?"

"Very well then. Be here at our studios, room 4B at six forty-five p.m. next Thursday." instructed Mr. Strausburg. "And don't be late. I don't tolerate people who are late, and they don't make good dance students, either."

"I understand. We'll be there," assured Lily.

The following day, Lily called Elliot and told him about the class. The dates and times were fine with him. When Thursday rolled around, Elliot picked up Lily at her home around six o'clock in the evening, and they drove over to the dance studio.

They found room 4B easily and were greeted at the door by Mr. Strausburg. He did not look at all like what Lily had pictured judging from his voice on the telephone. He had a very slight build. He had an angular face that was highlighted by well-kept salt and pepper hair and a handlebar mustache that he constantly stroked as he spoke.

"Good evening, I am Willem Strausburg, your Viennese waltz instructor. Come in please."

He was dressed in a dark gray, loosely-fitting jump suit and black and white sneakers.

Lily thought. *Hmm ... what have we gotten ourselves into? He doesn't look much like a dance instructor to me.*

She would soon come to realize that you cannot always judge a book by its cover.

Mr. Strausburg pointed to a row of straight-back chairs lined up against the large windows at the rear of the room.

He put his hand in the middle of Lily's back, gave her a firm nudge in the direction of the chairs and said, "Go ... sit there."

Then, pointing to Elliot, he said, "You, young man, stand up right here beside me and do not move until I tell you to do so."

Elliot took his place and stiffened up like a figure in a wax museum.

"Okay, Elliot ... it is Elliot, is it not?" Questioned Mr. Strausburg.

Elliot nodded in the affirmative.

"Take a deep breath and let it out very slowly." Mr. Strausburg looked back at Lily in her chair and barked, "Sit up straight, young lady and listen to the music in the background. Concentrate and you will hear it."

Lily sat up, but she could hardly hear the sound coming from an old phonograph player in the back corner of the room.

"I said listen." snorted Mr. Strausburg. "You must concentrate on nothing but the music. Block out everything else. Close your eyes if you must."

She finally could make out the beautiful sound of an orchestra playing Johann Strauss's "Vienna Waltz." The more she concentrated, the better she could hear the melodious tune.

Mr. Strausburg stood silent for almost two minutes.

Elliot looked at him as if to ask, "Okay, what do I do next?"

Mr. Strausburg looked him straight in the eye, put his hand to his chin, then gave Elliot the shush signal with his forefinger in front of his pursed lips. Then he wiggled it side to side to stop any audible inquisition from Elliot.

After a few more moments went by, Mr. Strausburg finally broke the silence. "Now, we start the lesson! Come over here, Miss Lily."

He motioned for her to stand back to back with Elliot.

The phonograph dropped another record onto the turntable. It began to play "Three Coins in the Fountain". Mr. Strausburg went over to the phonograph and turned up the volume so they both could hear it clearly. He then told Elliot to sway from his waist up (left and right) to the rhythm of the music. He told Lily to do the same but to only react to Elliot's movements. He was using this exercise to teach Elliot to lead and Lily to follow.

Elliot had no problem with the rhythm of the music or in translating it to the movement of his upper body, but Lily kept getting a little out of sync. She was with the tune's rhythm but was a split second off Elliot's pace.

Mr. Strausburg stepped in. "Okay, now face each other, please. Put your hands at shoulder height and touch your palms and fingers together. Do not interlock your fingers... just touch them. Now, Elliot, you begin with the music to lift your arms high and then swing them to the left and back to the right smoothly and to the rhythm of the music. Lily, you follow his lead."

Almost immediately, they began to synchronize their movements, and both smiled as if they were acknowledging their minor accomplishment.

"Stop and drop your hands to your sides." Mr. Strausburg instructed. "Do you get the concept of following and leading now?"

Lily and Elliot said, "Yes" in unison and they braced for the next set of instructions.

Mr. Strausburg became pensive again and just stood with his arms folded. With his head looking slightly downward, he lifted his eyes toward their eyes and told them that the waltz was by far the most romantic and fluid dances of all.

Then he summoned his wife, Eleanor, to his side with an outstretched hand. She had come in unnoticed and sat in the end chair during the last exercise.

Mr. Strausburg had Lily and Elliot stand to one side. He allowed the phonograph record to go to another piece of music.

Eleanor stood facing her husband with her arms out and palms down until he walked up to her gracefully. He placed his right hand in the small of her back and gently caressed her right hand with his left hand.

They began dancing with the basic steps; 1-2-3, 2-2-3, 3-2-3, 4-2-3 as he stepped toward her, she stepped back, etc.

They stopped after a few repetitions of those steps, and he said, "Now, the side steps." They did the same steps again but to the left and to the right.

They stopped again and Mr. Strausburg said, "Now, you just have to put it all together and add turns as you are traveling in a great circle. Watch the long strides, and our feet will just glide along the floor. Do not pick up your feet. We are not doing the barnyard strut … okay?"

Lily and Elliot watched in awe as the two masters seemed as though they were on skates.

Eleanor was a woman of elegance in her natural appearance, but when she was spinning in her husband's arms on the dance floor, she became a princess. She held her head sideways in the classic ballroom style that obviously came from endless hours of practice. Her floor-length pale green skirt flowed like a butterfly's wing. One end of it was held in her left hand the entire dance.

They continued until the end of the song. Eleanor walked over and took her seat.

Mr. Strausburg walked over to talk to the young couple.

"That is how the basic waltz is supposed to look. Lily, did you notice the position of my wife's head?" He asked, "Do you think you both can do it?"

Lily and Elliot nodded, still a little dazed at the beauty of what they had just witnessed.

"Well then, let's continue." Mr. Stausburg said. "We begin with the forward and back steps. We will not use the music until you get the steps of each movement down pat."

He had them stand face to face, and he stood side by side with Elliot. "First, I do the steps ... 1-2-3, 2-2-3, 3-2-3, and 4-2-3. Now, do them with me, Elliot."

Elliot was surprised at how easily he did the steps with the instructor right there beside him. They repeated them five times, then while Mr. Strausburg counted cadence, Elliot did the steps alone. After a few iterations, he was doing it quite well and calling his own cadence.

"Now, Lily. You will not do the steps with me or by yourself. You will do them with your partner." instructed Mr. Strausburg. "Remember to follow him."

They came together, and Mr. Strausburg had to show them the proper hand positions before they did the steps. The exercises they did at the beginning were very effective, and they mastered the forward and back steps quickly and to Mr. Strausburg's satisfaction.

The needle on the vinyl record made a little static sound as it moved to the next waltz tune.

Mr. Strausburg said loudly, "Well, what are you stopping for? Keep going. I will tell you when to stop. Go ahead. Go ahead!"

Elliot and Lily did not mind the repetition of the steps they had learned, but they thought they were ready to go on to the next steps.

They began to dance as if they were tired of doing the basics.

Mr. Strausburg urged them on. "Do you think that Rome was built in a day? Well, a proper waltz was not either. Now, do it once more."

After the next tune ended, Mr. Strausburg walked over to the phonograph, lifted the needle arm from the record, and set it on its holder.

"Well, now I want you to just sit here in these two chairs. Lily, you here, and Elliot, you there. Hold your arms straight out to the side and imagine that they are moving waves of water. Begin moving them at your fingertips and let the movement ripple all the way to your neck and shoulders. Do not move your head. Lily, you tilt your head to the right and keep it there."

He had them do this with no music for several minutes, and then he started the phonograph again.

Elliot looked at Lily. She began to smile. She cut her eyes towards him without losing her pose, and he smiled with satisfaction back at her.

After the record came to the end, Mr. Strausburg came up to them from behind, put his hands on their shoulders, and told them that this was the end of the first session. "Be here tomorrow night at the same time. Good night."

On the way home, Lily and Elliot talked about how exhausting the lesson was, but they both felt that it was going to be worth every minute to get it right.

The next night, they were at the studio at six forty-five.

They were let in by Mrs. Strausburg. She told them that her husband would be there promptly at seven o'clock.

"Come in and sit here by me." she said. "I want to tell you a little about my husband. You see, Willem was a great pianist a long time ago. He was a child prodigy and was destined to be perhaps the greatest classical pianist in the entire world.

I met Willem at the Conservatory in Vienna, Austria. I was studying art and wanted to be a great painter. We were married after we finished our studies and lived in Vienna for many years.

One day, when he was twenty-two, he took a break from practicing and went over to the giant windows of the conservatory. He had studied there before we were married and often went there to play after classes were over for the day.

The window was opened wide. He placed his hands on the window sill and stood there breathing in the refreshing autumn air. Suddenly, the window came crashing down on Willem's fingers. It crushed every one of them except for his thumbs.

After three operations on his hands, the doctors told him that he would never again be able to play the piano as he did before the accident. He was able to recover enough to do most of the everyday things he did with hands, but not the piano.

He was in state of depression for two years after that. Then, one evening, he was sitting in his chair by the fireplace at our home. He was listening to his music. I came over and took his hand and pulled him to his feet to dance with me. We danced many times in the following days and soon began to do it as a hobby. We took lessons just as you two are doing. We got better and better and started to compete.

And, do you know, that a year later, we became world champions in ballroom dancing? It was the tonic that we both needed. We were champions five times in all.

I am telling you all this to ask you to overlook Willem's crudeness. He really wants you to learn, so be patient with him and you will be just fine, okay?"

About that time, Mr. Strausburg came in the side door. He said hello and went straight to the phonograph. He put on a record that played only the melodious tapping of the waltz beat on a metronome.

He told Lily and Elliot to dance to the beat. He stood back and just observed them for the next three minutes, then told them to continue with the beat without the metronome.

After they finished, Mr. Strausburg had Eleanor come up with him. They demonstrated the turns again for them. He had Elliot and Lily join them, and they all practiced the basic steps and turns for the remainder of the lesson time.

"You still have a lot of work to do, but I am quite pleased with your progress. Next week, we will work on your posture," said Mr. Strausburg.

The next two weeks were strenuous for Elliot and Lily. They were not only practicing the waltz, but they were preparing for all the other things associated with the wedding which was quickly approaching. They persevered, and on the last day of lessons, they came to the studio and were greeted by Mr. Strausburg.

"Now, I have a surprise for you," he said as he walked over to the west wall of the studio.

He grabbed a wrought iron handle and pulled back a sliding panel, revealing a giant wall mirror that stretched from the ceiling to the floor and wall to wall.

"And now, I want you to see what you look like when you are dancing a proper waltz."

He started the music, and Lily and Elliot floated through the early steps and then the turns. As they began to move in the classic big circle, Eleanor and Willem joined them.

Elliot and Lily had become very good at the dance and were pleased with how they looked in the mirror, but they could see the obvious differences in the smoothness and polish between what they were doing and what their instructor and his wife were doing.

Mr. Strausburg told them that he was very proud of them for not only working so hard to learn the dance but for wanting to do such an "old-fashioned" dance at their wedding.

"Eleanor and I have enjoyed having you, and we wish you all the happiness. We ask that you promise that you will always dance with each other." He looked at Eleanor and pulled her close to his side.

Lily and Elliot responded by telling them how much they enjoyed the lessons and assured them that they would continue to dance.

As they left the studio, they looked back. Lily gave a waist-high wave, and they drove home with a sense of pride. Their focus shifted back to the wedding that was drawing nigh.

Chapter 19

The Wedding

It was May 6. The church was richly but simply decorated with a large arbor similar to the one in Elliot's garden. There were four rows of roses around the arbor. Each row consisted of a different color or variety of roses. Each corner of the pews along the middle aisle of the church was cradled by solid white roses.

The bridesmaids wore pink evening gowns with red satin sashes, white high heels, and had white ribbons in their hair.

Johnny wore a white tuxedo with a black bow tie. His boutonniere was one red rose in his lapel. Mr. Owens was dressed similarly to Johnny. He waited in the foyer of the church for Lily. Mrs. Owens sat in the front row to the left of the pulpit next to Mrs. Timberlake. They both were radiant. Mrs. Timberlake had on a full-length sequined gown that shimmered with every slight movement she made. Mrs. Owens also wore a full-length evening gown. It was pale yellow with a lace bodice and trim all around. It was obvious where Lily and Elliot got their good looks.

Lily's natural beauty was all the more enhanced by the stunning, full-length wedding gown. It was adorned with sequins and rhinestones that created curvi-linear scroll designs all over the dress. They formed a V-shape that started at her shoulders and came to a point about waist high in the back.

The high bodice in the front was accented by sequins that continued around the entire dress. Layers of lace overlapped three times halfway to the floor. The train was four feet long after it leveled off at the floor and trailed four feet behind her. It was designed in such a way that the ridges running lengthwise stayed perfectly in place with rhinestones bordering the end.

The bodice was highlighted by a modest neckline that came to a gentle curve at the bottom and continued up to her shoulders. The openings at the shoulders revealed Lily's slightly tanned but incredibly smooth, creamy skin.

The sleeves were full-length and tight to her arm down to the ruffled sleeves that flared out with silk and lace at her wrists.

Lily stepped out into the foyer to join her father. Mr. Owens was about six feet tall and had an athletic physique that he kept by working out almost every day. He wilted like a leaf, when he caught his first glimpse of his daughter coming toward him.

Lily walked up to him and rested her head on his chest. "Dad, you are the best father anyone could ever want." she whispered.

He replied, "Lily, you are the most beautiful, smartest, and most considerate daughter any father could ever have. I am so happy for you."

She wiped away a tear from his left eye and took his arm as he offered it to her.

As they started down the aisle, the "Wedding March" music began to play.

It took a few paces for them to get in step with the slow, methodical rhythm of the march and with the flower girls sprinkling rose petals before them, but by the time they reached the altar, they were perfectly synchronized.

Reverend Johnson looked at them both and said, "Who gives this bride away?"

Mr. Owens answered, "Her mother and I do." He took her hand and put it in Elliot's and stepped back one step and to one side, standing silent.

Reverend Johnson acknowledged the presence of everyone, and after asking if there was anyone present who could offer a reason why Elliot and Lily should not be married, he pulled out the poem that Elliot had given him a couple of weeks before the wedding. The name of the poem was "The Locket".

It read:

The vows of this, your wedding day
Are more than wishes you both will say ...
More than words constructing this rhyme;
They are bright ornaments suspended in time;
Decrees that can cement and solidify
Lasting covenants you can never deny.
Keep them sacred as you live every minute
Like a shining locket that has love within it.
Open it very often and with great care.
Firmly hold and protect all that is in there.
Seal it tightly with a solemn, true prayer,
Caress the contents, but most of all ... share.

He paused for the words to sink in completely and continued with the wedding ceremony.

At the end he said boldly, "I now pronounce you husband and wife. Elliot, you may now kiss the bride."

Elliot lifted the veil and kissed Lily gently.

Reverend Johnson concluded, "I now present to you Mr. and Mrs. Elliot Timberlake."

They turned, joined hands, and walked quickly out into the foyer of the church. They walked back down the hallway that led to the fellowship hall and got into place in front of the great banquet table to greet everyone. The table was spread with vegetables and fruits from Elliot's garden, and meat dishes ranging from baked ham to a perfectly prepared beef roast.

There was one person who did not go back to the reception room right away. It was Elliot's mother.

Ms. Timberlake hesitated before going back to the reception. She stayed in the sanctuary and sat on a pew about halfway down the aisle. She thought about her marriage to Elliot's father and the little poem resonated through her head over and over for several minutes. Suddenly, she began to cry. She lowered her head and put it in her hands. She tried to compose herself before going back to the fellowship hall.

There was a secret that she had vowed to keep when her husband died in that terrible car accident almost ten years ago. The vow she made was that Elliot would never find out that his father had left that night in a violent rage after confronting her about an affair she was having with someone in Eldsboro.

She had said some things to her husband that night that she was still carrying around to this day. She could not stop him from leaving that night. Too late, she discovered that she really did love him and that it would be very, very hard to live without him and to take care of her son by herself.

When she heard the poem, all the nightmares of that night and the following years flooded her heart again.

For her son's happiness, she had to keep the secret from him. When Elliot came back looking for her, she told him that she was just crying because she was so happy for him. She also admitted that the whole ceremony had brought back some happy and sad memories about his dad.

Elliot escorted her back to the reception and convinced her to have some food.

Mr. Owens had the first dance with his daughter. He had picked out a song called "Turn Around" was one that fitted the occasion perfectly. Still more tears came to his eyes when the phrase of the song "Turn around and you're a young girl going out of the door" was sung.

He led her over to Elliot when the song ended. He had been standing there waiting for his turn to dance with Lily. Their song was "Two for the Road" sung by Ed Ames, who was Elliot's favorite singer.

They had practiced their waltz several times with that song and their instructor, Willem Strausburg allowed them to dance to it at their next-to-last practice at the studio. They began all alone on the dance floor. The lights were low all around, but there was a spotlight in the center of the floor with blue lights illuminating several spots in a circle around the outside of the floor.

They thought of Mrs. Strausburg and his wife as they began to do their turns. They continued around the outer circle formed by the blue light reflections on the floor. Lily's head was tilted as she was taught, and Elliot led her exquisitely to the beat of the music.

As they continued, two other couples joined them in the circular part of the dance, and it was a sight to behold. Then, others came onto the floor doing slow dancing in every style imaginable, but Lily and Elliot did a proper waltz to the end.

Mrs. Owens joined her husband for that dance, too.

Then, it was time for the bride and groom to leave for their honeymoon.

Johnny called everyone to order and offered a toast. "To my great sister and my new best friend, have a happy, happy life, stay together as that song just said when you were dancing, 'travel down the road, collecting precious memories, selecting souvenirs, and living life the way you please'. Have a wonderful marriage!"

Everyone touched glasses and hugged one another.

Lily turned her back to the crowd and sent her bouquet flying over her head.

As luck would have it, none of the bridesmaids or other young girls caught it. Instead, it landed squarely in the outstretched hands of Mrs. Timberlake, who only reached out when she saw it heading her way. She looked at it for a moment in utter surprise, then lifted it high over her head.

Her face lit up and a big, beautiful smile came to her countenance.

She thought. *Maybe this is a sign that my secret will remain just that forever.*

Lily and Elliot went back to Elliot's house (now their home) to change for the trip. There were no tin cans attached to Elliot's truck, but someone had written "Just Married" on the back windshield in big white letters. An hour later, they were off to the airport in Columbus and on from there for a two-week stay in the Bahamas.

After a storybook trip, they would return to Eldsboro a bit tired but ready to get on with an equally wonderful life full of children, work, dancing, and a long life together.

While they were in the Bahamas, Mary Crenshaw and Ricky came back to town to collect the remainder of their belongings.

Mrs. Timberlake was still staying in Eldsboro at Elliot's house. While she was there, she got a call from Mary Crenshaw. She wanted to talk to her before she and Ricky went back to Florida.

They met at the coffee shop where Mary had worked. They sat down at a table near the window facing the street.

Mary said, "I appreciate you meeting with me, Mrs. Timberlake. There is something I thought you should know, before we part company for good."

"Okay, Mary ... go ahead, but I don't know what you could possibly have to tell me that is so important." replied Mrs. Timberlake.

Mary said, "Well, here goes. As you no doubt know, Dan Felton and I dated for quite a while several years ago."

"Yes, I remember that from the trial."

"Of course, but there is something more ... something that no one knows but me. I have never told anyone ... not even Ricky. I will never tell him, but I felt you had a right to know." Mary said.

"Please get to the point, Mary. I have to leave this afternoon to go back home." Mrs. Timberlake pleaded.

"Okay, Dan Felton confided in me that he had an affair with a married woman before he met me some years ago." Mary said.

Mrs. Timberlake's head dropped. She suddenly knew what Mary was about to reveal.

Mary continued, "He told me that it was you. Then he told me about your husband's car crash."

Mrs. Timberlake looked up and asked, "So, I guess you are going to blackmail me now with this information, huh?"

"Oh, no ... no. I would never do such a thing." Mary said. "I just wanted you to know that it would never go beyond this conversation. I thought you might wonder if Dan had told me, and I wanted to put your mind at ease. I promise you that ... because of what Lily and I went through with Dan. It just seemed like the right thing to do. I wish you and those two young people nothing but the best. And, now I must go."

Mrs. Timberlake thanked Mary and accepted her motives for telling her about what she knew.

They went their separate ways. Mary kept her word. She and Ricky lived happily for the next fifteen years, until Mary passed away from cancer.

Mrs. Timberlake divided her time for the remaining twenty-one years between her home in Williston and visiting for long spells with Lily and Elliot in Eldsboro and babysitting her two grandchildren who came along within the first few years of their marriage.

She never forgave herself completely for her husband's death and always wondered if he had purposely driven his car off the cliff that night.

However, she was content and busied herself in the service of her son and his family. They, in turn, gave her a love to fill the emptiness that she thought would never be filled.

Lily and Elliot finally sat down with her parents soon after they returned from their honeymoon and told them all the sordid details about the extortion that Felton had perpetrated against Lily and others. Lily's parents had made it a point not to press her about those details, but there had been many instances when Mr. Owens had told his wife that he was going to find a way to end that relationship.

But, in the end, he trusted his daughter's judgement. He knew that Lily had always done the right thing eventually. After all was said and done, he knew he had made the right decision. Lily had learned the lessons they taught her well.

At the sawmill, Elliot moved up the ladder and was assistant mill superintendent within a year. He gave up his thoughts of going into criminal law. He told everyone that he wanted nothing more to do with trials and police and lawyers. He just wanted to live a quiet life, go to work, see Lily every day, and commune with nature at every opportunity. He was not a super hero, but he turned out to be a great husband for Lily and a true hero to his children.

He did go through with buying the land he had shown Lily some time before and still hoped to build her a beautiful home overlooking the valleys and hills which, to him, were some of God's greatest creations.

In future years, a fly-by-night logging company decimated the forests lands adjacent to their acreage with clear-cutting. They left the land barren and did not even bother to replant or clean up the debris left behind. Elliot's company had been a leader in the industry and always had a policy of select cutting, cleaning up any debris, and replanting with the help of the people of Eldsboro and the surrounding towns and counties.

They never grew into a gigantic corporation, because they insisted on doing things that put the environment first. After all, it was the environment that gave them their livelihoods, so they maintained, conserved, and preserved the forests. They were rewarded with the respect of the whole state of Ohio and never had to venture beyond their original tracts of land to get their raw materials. It was a classic example of a win-win situation for everyone.

Most of the lumber companies of the area, including the one that owned the Eldsboro Lumber Mill, were conscious of the environment, but that one stripped every bit of life out of the land.

Elliot and Lily decided to leave their tract of land just as they found it and would one day donate it the Wildlife Conservancy of Columbus as a nature preserve.

He decided to keep his smaller farm closer to town. He used it as his hobby garden. The house would serve them just fine until he could build the new one. Lily loved the little farm. She was constantly reminded of the day she and Elliot met every time she went into the garden to herd him into the house for lunch or supper. Now, she could go out on her own to harvest some vegetables for his favorite meal of lima beans and tomatoes.

Author's Note

There is no real super hero in my story. For, you see, super heroes don't really exist except in comic books, novels, and movies. True champions of life are those people who love deeply and work diligently to serve those around them. Life is filled with people of integrity. There are those who wish us harm because of their own selfishness, but the winners in life are those who take one day at a time and cherish their families and friends.

Hate is not the ultimate victor in the grand scheme of things. Love is!

Love, kept in secret is one of the great injustices we can create for ourselves. It deserves to be open and free to flow through our veins and beyond to others.

It needs to be passed down through the generations of our history.

You see ... love is so strong that it cannot be broken down within the solution of time. It is multiplied and solidified by each person who shares in it with us.

The one who initiates love becomes fortified exponentially with each person who is added to the list of recipients.

When it comes to that demise that is imminent in all our lives, there is a treasure left behind as an inheritance that dwarfs any monetary wealth that we could possibly leave for our heirs.

About the Author

Jim Stratton was born on December 25, 1947 in Hartsville, South Carolina. His parents were James E. and Nellie Stratton. He has one brother, Doyle, who still lives in Hartsville. He has one daughter, Dr. Jennifer Do who lives in Little Rock, Arkansas with her husband, retired U.S. Army captain, Vuong Do.

Jim is married to Rebecca, and they reside in Florence, South Carolina. Rebecca has two daughters. Elle Poindexter lives in Portland, Oregon, and Emily Pearson lives in Missouri.

Imminent Demise is Jim's sixth book and his first novel. His first book was *View from My Easel* (poetry and prose) published in 1997. His second was *Waist Deep in Broom Sedge* (poetry, essays, and short stories) published in 2009. His third was *Screams and Whispers; The Life and Times of a Southern Artist* (his memoirs) published in 2014. His fourth was *Tod the Tadpole Grows Up* (a children's book) published in 2018. His fifth was *And Another Door Opens* (poetry, prose, and songs) published in 2018.

Jim graduated from Hartsville High School in 1966. He joined the United States Air Force in 1966 as an illustrator and served until 1970. He graduated from Florence-Darlington Technical College with an Associate Degree in Drafting and Design Technology in 1972, and worked as a sports editor and staff artist at the Darlington County Tribune from 1972 until 1974. He worked for Sonoco Products Co. in Hartsville from 1974 until he retired in 2009. He also has a certificate of graduation from Art Instruction Schools in Commercial Art.

During his time at Sonoco, he earned his Bachelor of Arts degree from Coker College in Hartsville. He has been painting in oils on canvas for more than fifty years and taught community interest classes in painting, drawing, and perspective.

Jim is a volunteer docent at the Florence County Museum of Art, History, and Science.

Printed in the United States
By Bookmasters